STALK THE NIGHT

THE ENFORCERS

JANE HINCHEY

BAYWOLF PRESS
BP
BAYWOLF PRESS

AUTHOR'S NOTE

Welcome to "The Enforcers" series—a collection that has truly been on a remarkable journey. When I first embarked on this adventure, I could hardly have imagined the twists and turns it would take. Initially self-published under my own name, these stories found a new identity with the pen name Zahra Stone, and even underwent a title transformation along the way. Now, they've come full circle, returning to their original author.

While I'm predominantly known for my cozy mysteries, "The Enforcers" holds a special place in my heart. It's a series that has evolved with me and witnessed the various stages of my writing career. I'm thrilled to present these stories to you once more, enriched by their journey and under my own name again.

To stay updated with all my literary escapades, including the latest on "The Enforcers" and my cozy mysteries, I warmly invite you to sign up for my newsletter. It's the best way to keep in the loop about new releases and exclusive content.

You can sign up for my newsletter here:

Janehinchey.com/subscribe

Thank you for joining me on this incredible journey. I hope you enjoy the world of "The Enforcers" as much as I have enjoyed bringing it to you.

xoxo

Jane

ABOUT THIS BOOK

Escaping your demons? Easier said than done, especially when yours revels in the swelter.

Picture this: a fire demon inside you, not just any fire demon, but one that thrives in blistering heat. That's my daily battle. So, why live in a frying pan? I chose the icy calm of Alaska to keep my fiery companion on ice. Until now.

Grandma's gone, and her last wish drags me back to Maxxan, Texas—my own personal inferno. Each scorching day is a fight to cage the beast within. I'm counting the seconds until I can flee this heatwave, back to my arctic sanctuary. But plans have a way of going up in flames.

Enter a SIA agent, as sizzling as the Texan sun, gunning to enlist me in his vampire eradication squad. He thinks I'll stay for the hunt; he doesn't know my vampire-slaying days are long behind me, a childhood memory at five.

The heat's on, my inner demon's stirring, and Maxxan's secrets are starting to simmer. Welcome to my firestorm. Welcome to Texas.

Author's Note: Welcome back to the world of Stalk the Night, originally released as Thirst for Fire, part of the SIA series under my name, Jane Hinchey. It ventured into the literary realm as Zahra Stone's Stalk the Night, but now it's time for its homecoming. While this edition hasn't undergone substantial edits, it's been lovingly revisited and re-released under my true name. Rejoin this supernatural journey, where the familiar meets the renewed, and the adventure continues with the same spirited essence.

I had to hand it to Grandma—her trump card was pretty epic. She'd been trying to get me to return home to Maxxan for years, and I was adamant it wasn't going to happen. Then she pulled this. Her trump card. She died. Now here I was traveling in a bus that reeked of body odor, mostly mine, and stale junk food, also mostly mine, on my way home to the one place on earth I did not want to be, to attend her funeral.

Resting my forehead against the window, the vibrations of the engine jarring me, I peered outside. We'd just passed the Maxxan city limit sign. Population twenty-one thousand, one hundred and eighty-two. Three long days, three different buses, four thousand miles. All bringing me back to the town that hated me. The town I'd sworn I'd never return to.

Maxxan is hot, just the way fire demons like it. Only I had always had trouble controlling my demon and had left Maxxan just before my eighteenth birthday — not of my own volition. The judge decided I was certifiably insane, and I'd been incarcerated in the Spirit Fields Psychiatric Institution for three long years. When they finally released me, I'd fled to Fairbanks, Alaska, the coldest place I could find. My plan? To keep my demon frozen. For if it loved the heat, it would surely hate the cold. And I'd been right. In Fairbanks, I'd led a relatively normal life. Until now.

On the empty seat next to me was the heavy coat I'd worn when initially boarding the bus in Fairbanks. It had been dark, but then we got very few hours of daylight. Already I missed the white landscape, the crystal forests, the biting cold. The air conditioner on the bus battled with the heat. The farther we moved into Texas, the hotter it got. I may as well have been traveling to Hell.

Navigating through the streets, the bus eventually pulled into the depot, a run-down gray building that was one lit lightbulb away from looking abandoned. The bus rumbled into the parking lot, drawing to a halt with a shudder and groan. The door swung open with a hiss, and the driver stood.

"Maxxan, Texas," he announced. Sweat stained his once-crisp shirt, leaving dark patches under his arms. He looked from me to outside and back again.

"Thank you," I replied. I was the only one disembarking here, which wasn't unusual when you were in the ass-end of nowhere. Grabbing my backpack and coat, I made my way down the aisle, nodded at the driver, and stepped down onto the rough surface of the parking lot.

"Looks like you have a welcoming party," the driver said.

"I wouldn't expect anything less." For there on the sidewalk, leaning against a post, arms crossed over his chest, was the sheriff. Why wasn't I surprised? I'd never had a good relationship with law enforcement, and they clearly knew I was returning. What did take me by surprise was suddenly being grabbed from behind and swung face-first into the side of the bus, a male voice shouting in my ear, "Hands against the bus, Shelton! Don't move!" and then being frisked.

"Are you fucking kidding me?" I could see the sheriff from the corner of my eye, saw him shake his head and straighten up before calling out to his deputy, "That's enough, Harvey."

"What? But, Sheriff, it's her! That Shelton girl. You said she was trouble."

"Deputy." The growl from the sheriff was low, but held authority. The deputy released me, stepping back and looking to his boss for instruction. He was new; he had that fresh, eager-to-please vibe about him. But the sheriff, I remembered him well. We had not parted on good terms, maybe because I'd put laxatives in his coffee that one time. Or was it twice?

"Errr, any luggage?" The bus driver cleared his throat and stuck his head out the door.

"Nope. This is it." I kicked the backpack I'd dropped when the deputy had pounced on me. "Won't be staying long."

"Okay, ma'am. Good luck." The door hissed shut, and the engine revved before beeping, indicating he'd put the bus into reverse. Slinging my backpack over my shoulder and scooping my jacket from the ground, I stepped onto the sidewalk out of the bus's path.

"We don't want any trouble here." The sheriff stepped in front of me, halting my progress. I blew out a breath.

"Am I being charged with something? Because riding that bus was punishment enough." Sarcasm dripped from my tongue. It was a natural talent, one that continually got me into more trouble than I'd care to admit.

"Apologies for his over-enthusiastic greeting." The sheriff bowed his head. As if that made everything better. As if they hadn't been waiting for me for a reason.

"Say what you need to say and then get out of my way. I've got places I need to be."

"Problem here, Sheriff?" Glancing up, I saw sex on two legs walking towards us. Suddenly, Maxxan got a whole lot more interesting. The newcomer approached, casual in jeans, work boots, a button-down shirt, and a baseball cap. But there was an air of authority about him, and my internal antenna started going berserk. He was law enforcement, had to be. He stopped, standing between the sheriff and me, so close I could smell him, and he smelled delicious. Musk and chocolate. He was tall, over six feet, with broad shoulders and muscular arms. His hair was obscured by his hat, but what I could see of it was brown. His eyes were hidden behind sunglasses, his jaw clean-shaven. I finished cataloging him, and I felt my lips curl in a smirk. A sexy lawman. Maybe things in Maxxan had changed after all.

"We don't want any trouble here, and from what I remember, she's trouble with a capital T." The sheriff puffed, his cheeks taking on a lovely pink hue.

"I'm sure she's not here to cause trouble." The man cocked his head to one side, studying me. "Are you?"

"Not on purpose." I couldn't make any promises. Trouble did have a tendency to follow me around.

"I'll take it from here, Sheriff." The man dismissed the sheriff and his deputy, and judging by both men bristling at the dismissal, I could only assume this guy who'd just taken hold of my elbow and was guiding me out of the bus depot was superior to them.

"SIA Agent Jordan Buchanan." He introduced himself, flashed a badge from his wallet before shoving it back into his jeans' rear pocket.

"SIA? What's that? A cousin to the CIA?" I tugged my arm out of his grip, and he let me go, keeping pace easily by my side as I headed down the street. Already the heat of the day pounded down on us, and I worked up a sweat.

"Supernatural Investigation Agency," he replied.

I stopped. Supernatural Investigation Agency? What the ever-living hell?

"That's a thing now? Because, you know, they had me committed. They had me sent away. For telling about the vampires." I narrowed my eyes and looked him over again. Was he a nutjob, like me, or was he taking the piss? I couldn't decide.

"Yeah, it's a thing. Only it's not a thing most people know about. Take the local law enforcement, for example. They don't know what SIA stands for, only that I'm in town working on a case, and they're to give me their full cooperation."

"Are you shitting me?" This sounded too far-fetched, even for me.

"Nope. I know about you, Rae." The way he said it, complete confidence that he knew me upside down and inside out, had me bristling. I felt a momentary pang of sympathy for the sheriff and his deputy.

"You know nothing about me, Agent." I began walking again. I didn't like this, not one bit.

"I know you're a fire demon," he said conversationally. I glanced around to make sure no one had heard him. Thankfully, the streets were pretty empty.

"Part. Part fire demon," I mumbled.

"And I know you killed a vampire when you were five."

"I did no such thing." How the fuck did he know this stuff? My heart rate picked up; my skin tingled. My demon was stirring, picking up on my agitation. The bloody heat wasn't helping either. Clenching my fists, I ignored the small zap of static electricity that shot out.

"I know your cousins are also fire demons, but none of them have the unique abilities you do."

"Listen." I spun, placing my hand against his chest, halting him. "I don't know where you got this bullshit from, but it ends here and now."

"Deny it all you like, Rae. You don't think the SIA knows about *all* supernaturals? Just because you've never heard of us doesn't mean we don't exist."

"Why are you telling me this? I won't be staying long. I'm here for my grandmother's funeral, and then I'm outta here. I don't want to be in this godforsaken pit hole any more than the townsfolk want me here, so let's end this little charade, hmmm? I don't have the time."

Spinning on my heel, I walked away. I had a funeral to get to. One I didn't relish. I'd been keeping a tight lid on the grief that was waiting for me, didn't want to think about Grandma, remember the good times, for after the good memories came the bad. Fingers wrapped around my wrist in a steely grip, halting me, and I looked down at the tanned fingers against my white skin and then back up at SIA Agent Jordan Buchanan. He released me as if I'd burned him. Which I could have if I wanted to.

"I need your help," he said.

"For what?"

"People are being killed. We think it's vampires."

"You're the one working for the supernatural fancy pants agency," I taunted. "I suggest you do something about it. Pretty sure you don't need little old me getting in the way."

"You're right. Vampires I can deal with. But there's something else." Oh, how I wished he hadn't said that, for immediately, I was intrigued. Something else besides vampires? I opened my mouth to demand he tell me everything, then closed it with a snap. No, I scolded myself. I am not staying. Don't get involved. And don't trust this man—if he's who he says he is, where was this agency when I was labeled crazy and locked away?

"You laid hands on me. As did the sheriff's deputy. With no cause. That could be classified as assault at the worst, intimidation at the least. I'm not here to put up with your shit. And believe me, if this harassment continues, you'll get more than you bargained for with me."

"Is that a threat?" He sounded incredulous, and I laughed out loud.

"A promise," I said under my breath, not caring if he heard or not. SIA Agent Jordan Buchanan may be one sexy lawman, but one thing still remained. All lawmen were assholes who abused their power. I didn't know what game he was playing with all this talk of vampires and other things, but I couldn't let myself get dragged into it. I had a plan, and it was imperative I stick to it for my own sanity if nothing else.

I had misjudged Agent Buchanan. I'd fully expected him to let me walk away. Instead, he'd hurried to catch up, once more matching his long strides to my shorter ones.

"It would go easier on you if you cooperated," he said. I ignored him. I could feel the sun burning my arm. I held it out to see a light tint of red staining my pasty white skin.

"You're burning." He stopped, grabbing my wrist once again and examining my arm. I ignored the way my skin tingled from his touch, telling myself it was my demon getting riled up. "Come on." Tugging me with him, he did an about-face, steering us back toward the bus depot. Parked out the front was a big, black SUV.

"Subtle." I snickered. I'd decided to save my own skin and let him give me a ride. It was, after all, bloody hot and I was no longer accustomed to the conditions. Once I'd had tanned skin and rarely burned. Now I was sweating like a pig and figured I looked a sight.

"Was that so hard?" he said under his breath, sliding in behind the wheel and starting the engine. Cool air immediately blew through the vents, and I adjusted them to blow in my face.

"Look, Agent." I swiveled my head to look at him, taken aback momentarily by how handsome he was. It had been a while since I'd had a lover. Clearly, I was in need. "If this Agency of yours really does exist, then I'm sure you have all the resources you need to deal with Maxxan's vampire problem. You don't need me."

"Your grandma said you were stubborn." Pulling out from the curb, he kept his attention on the road, missing the sight of my mouth dropping open and my eyes widening.

"You know Grandma? Knew," I corrected myself. I still couldn't fathom that she was gone. I couldn't even bear to think about it lest the pain consume me.

"Yes, ma'am."

"Don't call me ma'am."

"Okay."

"How did you know her?"

"Researching fire demons led me to her. She had a lot to say about you. She's the one who convinced me you could help."

A wave of exhaustion swept over me. Tired of the conversation, I turned my head to stare out the window. Agent Buchanan didn't need directions; he knew precisely where Grandma's house was. I was grateful he'd followed my lead and had shut up about the vampires. My mind was spinning enough as it was, and dread was starting to build at the thought of facing my family once more.

All too soon, we pulled up outside the big old house a few miles out of town. Flinging open my door, I tossed an offhanded "thanks" over my shoulder, relieved when he didn't follow me out of the SUV, instead merely nodding his head and then driving away as soon as I'd slammed the door shut. I stood looking at the two-story plantation-style home that needed a lick of paint. This house held so many memories, both good and bad. It had been the start of it all, but that was one memory that wasn't going to see the light of day, not today.

The front gate squeaked as I pushed it open and

headed down the path toward the front door, which stood open. I could hear voices inside, knew most, if not all, of my family were already gathered here. My grandparents had three sons, all of whom had married and provided them with eight grandchildren in total. I was the eldest, had meant to be an example to the others. More like an example of what not to do, I thought with a grimace. I longed to see my family, yet I was hesitant. So much had changed.

Climbing the steps to the veranda that provided welcome relief from the sun, I wiped the sweat from my face with the back of my arm, cringing at the stench of perspiration coming from my armpits. There had been no opportunity to shower in the three-day journey to get here, and I was sorely in need.

"Rae! You made it!" I was pulled into my mother's embrace and squeezed until I thought I'd pop. Familiar perfume filled my nostrils, and another wave of nostalgia claimed me. I'd missed my mom. I hadn't known it until now, breathing in her familiar scent, being pressed against her warm body.

"I told you I would." Clearing my throat, I stepped back. "Don't get too close, Mom, I stink."

"You do." She laughed, the sound joyous. "Come on upstairs and get freshened up. I'll let the others know you're here."

"So, they can settle up their bets?" I drawled.

"I'm going to get the jackpot." Mom laughed again, leading the way up the stairs. Grandma's house was massive, with six bedrooms on the second floor alone.

"You knew I'd come?" Why was I even surprised?

"Of course, darling. No matter what happened, we're family, and you've always done the right thing by family." I was pretty sure my family had disowned me after I'd been locked away. Mom had visited a few times, as much as they'd allowed—I'd kept getting my privileges, such as they were, revoked. I'd barely heard from the rest of my family since, and that was eight years ago. I hadn't seen Dad since they'd dragged me from the courtroom, kicking and screaming. Or my brothers Cameron and Tyler, although, since my release, we'd reconnected on social media.

"I made this room up for you." Mom opened a door, and I glanced inside. A big wrought iron bed with a yellow dandelion comforter took center stage.

"I'm staying here? In Grandma's house?" I

hadn't expected that. I'd thought I'd be going home. To Mom and Dad's. To my old room.

"I'm sorry, darling, but...well, once all you kids moved out, we did some renovations, and now your rooms aren't your rooms anymore. You don't mind, do you? There's not enough space at your brother's apartment."

"It's fine, Mom. Don't worry about it." Only it wasn't fine, and a twinge of anger, along with a jolt of fire, pulsed through my veins. Closing my eyes, I concentrated on centering myself, channeling the anger, and suppressing the fire.

"Rae?" Mom's hand on my shoulder had my eyes flying open.

"I'm going to shower, Mom, and then I'll be right down, okay? I'll be as quick as I can. I assume everyone's here, and you're all waiting on me." I refrained from adding the words "as usual" to the end of that sentence.

"We've got time." Mom glanced at her watch. "Another forty minutes before Father Moore arrives."

The brief flare of joy I'd felt at seeing Mom faded as quickly as it had arrived. Father Moore would be bringing Grandma. In a casket. To be buried up on the hill next to Grandpa. A shudder ripped through me, and I turned to the bed, throwing my backpack on it and digging inside for toiletries.

Flicking on the cold water tap in the shower, I held my hand under the spray, waiting in vain for the water to turn icy. The best I got was somewhat cool. Even the cold water ran hot in Maxxan. This was why Grandpa had settled and started his family here. The heat. He was a fire demon. Only when he'd chosen a human to mate and marry, his people had banished him, so he and Grandma had pulled out a map and chose the hottest place they could find that was still habitable, survivable for a human. Maxxan.

Shrugging out of my clothes and tossing them in a pile in the corner, I stepped under the spray, sucking in a breath as the water hit my overheated flesh. These days I was used to the cold, subzero temperatures. It would take time to adjust to the heat. But it didn't matter, I told myself, because once the funeral was over, I was out of here. I'd spend the night, for no more buses were leaving Maxxan today. Still, I had a ticket in my purse for eight tomorrow morning, and I had every intention of being on that bus. I just had to get through today.

"You're burned." My cousin Vanessa eyed me up and down, a frown pulling her brows together. "And fucking white."

Touching my fingers to my heated cheeks, I could feel the burn Vanessa mentioned. Too much sun on my almost virgin skin. Standing beneath the burning rays, we'd buried Grandma at noon. Beside Grandpa, beneath the big old tree on the hill. Then walked back to the house where the rest of the townsfolk had gathered to pay their respects.

"Not so much sunshine in Alaska," I said. I hadn't seen my cousins since before my trial. The family had kept the younger children away, not wanting me to taint them with my behavior. Or give them ideas of their own. Vanessa brought me up to date. She and her twin, Travis, had bought an advertising business in Redmeadows and were running it together.

"Your own business, eh?" I nodded, feigning interest. These people felt like strangers to me. My family, my own flesh and blood, were nothing to me. I felt no emotion toward them. I wasn't pleased to see them or displeased. I'd felt a brief flare when Mom had held me, but that had long since gone, and now I just felt empty inside.

Dad could barely meet my eyes. He'd looked me

up and down when I'd come downstairs in my figure-hugging black dress. It was the only dress I owned, and I felt self-conscious as fuck in it. Dad's eyebrows pulled together before he turned his back, and I had to stop myself from racing back upstairs and changing into my usual attire of jeans and a T-shirt.

"You could have made an effort," he'd snarled. I'd been taken aback, I admit.

"Me being here is an effort," I'd snapped back. And that had been the extent of our conversation. I'd always been my own person. I'd never conformed, no matter how much Dad had pushed. And he'd pushed. I'd spent more time grounded than at school.

"You did good today." Tyler, my youngest brother, slapped me on the back and grinned.

"I didn't do anything," I protested, confused.

"Exactly! Well done." He winked to show he was joking, and I relaxed a fraction.

"I thought Sophie would be here today." Sophie was Tyler's girlfriend, and from what I'd seen on Facebook, the pair were practically joined at the hip.

"She should be here any second. She didn't want to intrude on the service, but she'll be here for the wake."

"You're happy?" I asked, looking intently into his eyes, the dark brown an exact match to my own. He'd been fourteen when I'd been locked away, and a twinge of regret had my hand twitching, a crackle of electricity skimming over my skin.

"Yeah, I am. What about you, Rae? You got yourself a boyfriend locked away in the snow?"

I laughed. "In my basement, you mean?"

"That'll work." Tyler nodded. The banter with my brother eased my tension, soothing my demon. The pain of the funeral, of the tears that had fallen unheeded down my cheeks, the ache in my heart. My eyes had not been on Grandma's coffin but on Grandpa's headstone. He'd died saving me. It was my fault he was dead. Everything had turned to shit since that one pivotal point in time.

"Hey, Rae." Cameron, my other brother, pushed a beer bottle into my hand. "Get this into you."

"Thanks, Cam." Taking a swig, I let the cool alcohol soothe my tight throat.

"When you heading back?" he asked. "I assume you're not sticking around?"

"Tomorrow morning. I can't stay, Cam, you know that. This place is...bad for me."

"But you're okay now? Aren't you?"

"If you mean, do I have control? Then yes. I

have control. I'm fine. But I don't want to push the limits. None of us want my demon unleashed."

"Shhh, Rae." Vanessa waved a hand. "Don't talk about that here." She indicated the locals who were gathered in the house, standing in groups talking, sharing stories of Grandma, hovering by the buffet table, and hoovering up the morsels Mom delivered from the kitchen.

"Relax, don't get your G-string in a twist." It was out before I could stop it. Someone was always telling me what to do. I was done with it eight years ago, and I was done with it now. Turning my back, I wove my way through the crowd, nodding when people offered their condolences, noting the speculative way they looked at me, knew they were judging me, finding me lacking. Some things never changed.

Behind me, I could hear Cameron and Tyler arguing with Vanessa, telling her to get off my case, to leave me be, that she didn't understand. Vanessa and I were chalk and cheese. Vanessa had always followed the rules. Whereas I went out of my way to break them. Vanessa wore dresses and makeup. I wore jeans and boots and had unruly hair. We had never seen eye to eye, and I knew Vanessa would never truly understand the battle I had with my demon.

All of us were part fire demon, diluted now with human DNA. The family had speculated that I perhaps had a stronger proportion of demon than human since my demon was so strong within me. None of my cousins experienced the outbursts I did, the lack of control, the all-consuming fire. Not even my father, who was half fire demon himself, had such control issues.

The screen door slammed against the house as I busted through, and I cringed, hating that I was drawing attention to myself. Dragging in a deep breath, I grabbed the door and carefully closed it. *Stay calm*. At the far end of the verandah was the porch swing I'd loved as a child, and I made my way to it, gingerly sitting down, testing its weight in case I found myself on my ass.

I'd been alone, enjoying the solitude for all of ten minutes, when it was shattered by the sound of the back door opening and footsteps heading my way. My eyes were closed, and I'd let my head drop back, my mind drifting, doing my best not to think of anything. The footsteps were heavy, male. Not the tread of either of my brothers. A cousin, maybe? Besides Vanessa's twin brother, Travis, I had another cousin, Cody, a year younger than me. Squinting open one eye, I promptly closed it again when I saw who was standing over me.

"What are you doing here?"

I heard movement, assumed he was taking his hat off, could hear as he ran his fingers over the brim while holding it in front of him.

"Came to offer my condolences."

"Thanks. You can go now." I dismissed him. I wasn't interested in any of this social bullshit.

"It's a big moment for this town. The black sheep returns," he said.

"Jesus. Move along now, Buchanan."

"I meant what I said earlier, Rae. I need your help. This town needs your help. Your family needs your help. Haven't the ones you love suffered enough?"

"Probably."

Instead of leaving, he sat next to me, and my temper crept up a notch. *Keep control.* I could smell him again, that warm chocolate musk smell that tempted me to lick him to see if he tasted as delicious as he smelled.

"Where have you been, Rae?"

"Not here." I had a feeling he knew exactly where I'd been. Agent Buchanan had done his homework on me quite thoroughly. Maybe he was changing tactics, asking questions instead of revealing all he knew, in the hopes that I'd agree to help him. He'd have a long wait, I vowed silently.

"Thanks for the condolences, Agent." I left him sitting on the porch swing, could feel the heat of his gaze boring into my back as I went back into the house. If I wasn't leaving in the morning, I'd almost be tempted to hang around and see what game the agent was playing. Almost.

THREE

"I love you, Rae, but you're as broken as they come." Aunt Martha pressed a wad of notes into my hand. "Enough for a ticket back to Alaska."

"Gee, thanks, Aunt Martha." Curling my fingers around the cash, I didn't bother telling my aunt I already had a ticket bought and paid for. If my family was that desperate to get rid of me, let them shower me in cash.

"Everyone! Please gather around." Martha's husband, Glenn Shelton, clapped his hands, shushing the chatter. It had been a long day; the wake had lasted several hours, and now the sun was creeping over the horizon. The townsfolk had departed. All that was left was the family and the reading of the will.

"Thank you, Glenn." A middle-aged man dressed in a stiff black suit tugged at his tie and ran his finger around the collar. "I'm Curtis Jacobs, Rose Shelton's lawyer and executor of her will." He seemed agitated, and I wondered why. His eyes landed on me and danced away, sweat beading on his forehead. *Ah. Of course.* My presence made him nervous. Sighing, I took up a stance, leaning against the living room wall, arms crossed over my chest. Once this was over with, I could go to bed, get a good night's sleep, and in the morning, I'd be gone. Goodbye to the heat of Maxxan; hello to the snowy climate of Alaska. I grinned at the prospect.

"This is the last will and testament of Rose Alice Shelton, wife of Thomas Shelton, deceased, mother of Frank, Glenn, and Roy, grandmother to Raelene, Cody, Cameron, Vanessa, Travis, Paige, Katie, and Tyler."

I grimaced at the use of my full name. No one called me Raelene. Not since the judge in the stifling courtroom eight years ago. I hadn't thought of my stint at the Institute in such a long time, but now, being back in Maxxan, it was all fresh in my mind, as if it had happened yesterday. Tomorrow couldn't come quickly enough.

The lawyer droned on, talking about assets, heirlooms, bank accounts. It wasn't until my name was mentioned that I tuned back in.

"Raelene. Rae." The lawyer looked at me and then down at the paper in his hand. "There's a letter here that Rose has asked me to read." He cleared his throat, smoothed a trembling hand over the paper, then began.

"My darling Rae. We did wrong by you. In so many ways, too many times, we—us, your family— did wrong by you, and with the power of hindsight, I can see that now. Now, when it's too late to tell you in person. When it's too late to right the wrongs. Forgive me, my child.

Thomas's death was not your doing or your fault. It was, however, your trigger. Your coming of age should not have happened at the tender age of five. We did not see it, could not fathom the pain you were going through, unable to control the fire within you—a fire that should not have flared to life until your eighteenth birthday.

Instead, we treated you as a rebellious child and teenager. Punished you. Allowed you to be locked away. Let you be taken from us. Nothing in the world can make up for what was done to you. I can never convey how very sorry I am. Thomas would be ashamed of us all."

The lawyer stopped for a moment, cleared his throat, and ran a finger around his collar again but didn't look up. My breath had caught in my throat, and I waited, stunned at his words.

"Our family is fractured, and that is on me. I will see to it that we are whole once more. I daresay you will be angry with what follows, Rae. You will rebel — I'm counting on it. But know this. I love you. No matter what you did, no matter whose fault it was, I always have and always will love you."

You could have heard a pin drop; the room was so silent. All waiting. What had Grandma done? Folding up the letter, the lawyer held it out, eventually letting his arm drop when I refused to take it.

"Get on with it," I growled, moved by Grandmother's words but angry that this, her funeral, the day we said goodbye to her, had been made all about me. Again. I wanted to slink off to my room with a bottle of whiskey and forget it all.

"To Raelene Mary Shelton, I leave my house and the surrounding land."

"I don't want it," I cut in, but the lawyer looked at me and shook his head before continuing.

"On the provision that she lives in it for one full year. The property cannot be sold or handed to another."

"Are you fucking kidding me?" I pushed away from the wall and began pacing. "I don't want this house. I don't want to be here, and I'm pretty sure as shit none of you want me here."

"There must be provisions for if she doesn't live in the house?" Uncle Roy directed his attention to the lawyer.

"There are. She can live in the house for a year and then sell, and the proceeds will be shared between Raelene and her cousins."

"And if she doesn't live in it? If she refuses?"

"Then, after a year, the house will be sold with the proceeds going to a charity that will be disclosed at that time."

"How much? How much are we talking?" I asked, hating being backed into a corner this way.

"The house and land? Over a million. Probably closer to two, if not more," the lawyer replied. "Give or take. Depends on the market at the time of sale, but Maxxan is growing, and this land is prime real estate for future growth and development."

"No." I shook my head. This couldn't be happening. I was being blackmailed into staying. *Jokes on you, Grandma. I don't want your money.*

"Think of your cousins," Uncle Roy said. "They could use that money. So could you. Start afresh after a year. You'd all get, what, around one hundred and forty thousand each? At the very least. Van and Travis could use that for their business. Cameron could use it for his garage. Any one of you could buy a house. Anything."

"Forget the money," Travis said. "I don't want to sell the house. We need to keep it in the family." Vanessa nodded, and Katie and Paige joined in. *Fuck.*

"She's trapped me." I couldn't help but admire Grandma's tenacity. If I didn't live in the house, it would be sold, and none of the family would get the money. If I did live in the house, I could sell it and share the money with my cousins. But only after a year. And my cousins didn't want the house sold at all.

"What happens if I don't make it to a year? What happens if it falls short and I leave?"

"Then the house will be sold, and the proceeds go to charity. After a year."

"Think of someone other than yourself for a change," Dad said.

Mom jabbed him in the ribs with her elbow. "Frank. Did you just hear what your mother wrote? About how we should be supporting Rae? Rose is right. We allowed everything to happen. This is our fault, too. You can't put it all on Rae."

"Like hell, I can't." Dad stormed over to the dresser where the alcohol was kept and poured himself a whiskey. I could use one myself but was reluctant to join him unless I fancied being backhanded across the face. I could see the barely controlled violence in the trembling of his hand.

"When do I have to make a decision?" I asked the lawyer, pushing down the hurt at my father's continual rejection.

"You don't. Your actions will dictate what happens next. If you leave?" He gestured with one hand, "The house will sit empty for twelve months, and then I will arrange the sale. If you stay? Well, you decide at the end of the year what you want to do."

"So, I can't return to Alaska? At all? To get my things even?"

"No. You must not leave Maxxan at all for the next twelve months."

"Then I guess we'll find out tomorrow." Darting across the room, I snatched the bottle of whiskey and fled the lounge room, bounding up the stairs, two at a time, electricity dancing over my skin. *Trapped.* I was trapped. How could Grandma do this to me?

Slamming the bedroom door, I sank to the floor at the end of the bed, spun the lid off the whiskey bottle, and took a healthy gulp. It burned, but it was nothing compared to the fire my demon was igniting. I was tired. And hot. It was too hot to think. Think straight anyway. I could hear muted voices downstairs, most likely talking about me, about what this meant, for all of them. I couldn't stay. It simply wasn't an option. Which would mean this beautiful old house would sit empty for a year. Be neglected. Then sold. The neglect would affect the sale. But then, my cousins didn't want the house sold; they wanted it kept in the family. Maybe they could all pool together and buy it at a reduced price because it hadn't been maintained. I clung to that thought.

Someone knocked at my door, then banged. Mom called to me. More voices joined her. I ignored them all. Today had been shitty enough with my bizarre encounter with Agent Jordan Buchannan and his talk of vampires and fire demons. I'd never in a million years expected it to end like this. Slowly, the noise outside my door abated. They wanted to sway me, one way or the other. I didn't need swaying; my decision was made. In the morning, I'd be on the bus.

FOUR

"Want to ride on my back, sugarplum?" Grandpa asked, glancing down at my small hand curled around his. "We lost track of time, and Grandma is going to be mad at us if we're late for supper."

I giggled, then nodded. I loved walking in the hills with Grandpa, searching for mushrooms. He promised me they were out there, but we'd never found any. Ever. Only today, we'd walked a little further, and the sun had dipped over the horizon, twilight bathing the hills in shadows.

"Come on then. Jump up." He crouched, and I scampered behind him and jumped, wrapping my arms around his neck and my legs as far around his waist as I *could reach. He looped his elbows behind my knees to keep me anchored in place.*

It was soothing, being rocked as he walked, and I must have dozed off for the next thing I knew, I was flying through the air, landing hard on the ground.

"Ow." I whimpered, rubbing my elbow. It was dark now. Grandma would be mad. But...where was Grandpa? Peering through the darkness, I tried to find him but couldn't. I couldn't see anything. "Grandpa?"

"Run, sugarplum!" There. To my left. The sounds of grunting and shuffling.

"Grandpa?" I called again, struggling to my feet. I headed toward the sound.

"No, Rae! Run! Run as fast as you can. It's vampires!" Grandpa yelled. My eyes had adjusted to the dark now, and I could make out the shadow figures, three of them. One was Grandpa. But what did he mean, vampires? What was a vampire? I stood, uncertain. He wanted me to run. I recognized the urgency in his voice, and it finally penetrated that we were in danger. I had to get help. Turning, I ran.

"Not so fast, bambino!" I was swept off my feet by an arm around my waist. I screamed. Grandpa screamed my name in response, and then he was running toward me.

"You let her go!" he thundered, a shot of fire shooting

from his hand, lighting up the night. The man holding me darted to the side so fast my neck snapped painfully. The bolt of fire missed its mark. The other man, vampire, leaped onto Grandpa's back, opened his mouth wide, and then sunk his teeth into Grandpa's neck. Grandpa roared in pain, struggled to dislodge the vampire, the scent of blood heavy in the air.

The vampire holding me caught the scent of the blood and tossed me to the ground. I caught a glimpse of his glowing red eyes a second before he pounced on Grandpa, teeth ripping into his shoulder. Grandpa's head snapped back, mouth open to scream but no sound, only a strange gurgling noise, and I knew, I knew he was dying. They were killing him.

Struggling to my feet, I ran toward them, nothing but a child against two vampires in the throes of blood lust. I tugged at the vampire's leg, and he kicked me away. I slid along the ground several feet, my skin burning from the impact. Then a loud thud next to me, and I looked into the lifeless eyes of my grandfather.

"Grandpa?" I whispered, hand shaking as I reached for him, touched his face with my fingers, feeling tears wet my cheeks. "Wake up, Grandpa."

"Now for dessert." The vampire was looking at me, and I knew he meant to kill me, too. Rising to my hands and knees, I attempted to crawl away, but he caught my

ankle and hoisted me into the air, laughing at my cries as he held me upside down.

"You want first taste?" he asked his friend, laughing.

"Nah, you caught her. Go ahead."

"Children have the sweetest blood," he murmured, holding me effortlessly as I continued to twist and struggle, kicking out with my free leg. The blood was rushing to my head, and I felt strange. Then he bit me. His teeth sunk into the back of my calf, and I screamed, the sound long and loud and echoing through the hills. Pain shot through me, and I cried for my mom. For help. But no help was coming.

"Argh!" Unexpectedly, the vampire dropped me, clutching his throat. I fell to the ground in a heap, barely able to see for the tears in my eyes.

"What is it?" The other vampire rushed to his friend's side while the vampire who'd bitten me coughed and choked, foaming blood flying from his mouth. His blood or mine? While I was watching, something was happening to me. I burned. All over, inside and out, I felt like I was on fire, and it was excruciating. My insides were burning, lava pumping through my veins where once blood had traveled. The vampires were forgotten as I writhed on the ground, scream after scream torn from my throat. I felt like I was too big for my skin, that I would tear free from my

body. My last conscious thought was that I was going to die here with my grandpa. At least we'd be together. Then nothing, nothing but darkness as oblivion claimed me.

SITTING UP IN BED, I clutched at my chest, trying to suck in a breath. I was covered in sweat, my hair damp with it, the shirt I'd slept in soaked. I hadn't dreamed of that night in years, but being in this house brought it all back. Swinging my legs over the side of the bed, I sat, trembling. Right now, I'd give my left arm for some of the drugs they'd pumped into me at the asylum, for they numbed everything, took away the pain, the anger, the hurt. But I didn't have the drugs anymore. I'd gone cold turkey the day I walked out the gates, and I hadn't looked back, hadn't craved them. *Until now.*

Breathe. Inhaling through my nose and exhaling through my mouth, I focused on the simple act of breathing until my trembling stopped. A slightly hysterical laugh escaped for no apparent reason other than the ridiculousness of it all. Why had Grandma laid a trap for me? Why would she want me to stay? I was a lost cause. I knew it. Hell, everyone knew it. Why bother trying to change me now?

Reaching out, I wrapped my fingers around the whisky bottle on the bedside table. Taking a swig, I embraced the burn and welcomed the numbness it would eventually bring. If I couldn't block out the memories with drugs, alcohol would have to do. I sat on the edge of the bed and drank as if my life depended on it until the room began to bend and sway until the bottle was empty and slipped through my fingers to fall with a soft thud on the carpet. I flopped back onto the bed, staring up at the ceiling.

"Don't matter none, Grandma," I slurred. "I mean, kudos to you, great plan 'n all, but I'm not staying. In the morning, I'll be on that bus. Ain't nothin' you can do to stop it."

FIVE

"Are you kidding me?" Throwing my phone onto the bed in frustration, I watched as it bounced twice, then fell to the floor on the opposite side. "Fucking great." I'd forgotten to charge it, and now the battery was dead.

Cursing, I rounded the bed and scooped it from the floor, ignoring the throbbing in my head as I shoved it into the side pocket of my backpack. I'd been about to call a taxi to take me into town when I discovered the black, unresponsive screen. Backpack in one hand and coat in the other, I ran downstairs and into the kitchen, snatched the landline receiver from the wall, and listened for a dial tone. None was forthcoming. Damn it, they'd canceled Grandma's service already? How surprisingly efficient.

"I'm not staying, Grandma," I grumbled, rummaging in the kitchen drawers. "I know you think you've thought of everything, old woman, but you've underestimated me this time." Triumphantly, I pulled out a set of car keys and held them up, a grin on my face.

Outside, I wrestled the garage door open, then stood looking at the blue hatch covered in dust. The tires were low, but not totally flat. I figured I had enough air to get me into town. That's if I could get the car started. Clearly, Grandma hadn't driven it in a long time.

Climbing into the driver's seat, I tossed my backpack and coat onto the passenger seat and slid the key into the ignition. Closing my eyes on a prayer, I turned the key. Nothing. Total silence.

"No!" My yell echoed around the garage, the sound bouncing from wall to wall. Blowing out a frustrated breath, I popped the hood. One thing I remembered Dad always telling me—if you weren't going to drive a car for a period of time, disconnect the battery. I hoped that was the case here. Moving to the front of the car, I felt for the release catch, then lifted, closing my eyes for a quick, silent prayer before looking down into the engine bay.

"Eureka." Sure enough, the battery cables lay

across the engine, disconnected from the battery. Propping the hood open, I reconnected everything before slamming the hood shut. This time, when I turned the key in the ignition, the engine turned over, and with a couple of pumps on the accelerator, I managed to coax it into life. A rattling, coughing life, but the engine was running, and I just needed it to stay that way long enough to get me into town.

Throwing it into reverse, I backed out of the garage, squinting against the glare of the sun on the dusty windshield. Flicking on the windscreen wipers to try to disperse some of the dust, I slammed it into drive and peeled down the driveway, gripping the steering wheel tight as it fought me every step of the way.

Grandma's car was almost as old as Grandma herself, which meant no such thing as power steering or electric windows. For a small hatchback, it handled like a truck, and I broke a sweat manhandling the car around the corners. I was almost in town when flashing blue and red lights appeared in the rearview mirror.

"You have GOT to be kidding me!" Flipping on the indicator, I pulled over, my fingers gripping the steering wheel extra tight as electricity danced over my knuckles. *Breathe.*

"License and Registration." The Sheriff appeared at the window, hands-on-hips. I squinted up at him. He looked fresh in the early morning light, unlike me, who'd already worked up a sweat, and a quick glance at my dusty clothes told me I looked like I'd been rolling around on the dirt road.

"Sure." Leaning over, I punched the button on the glove box and dug around inside for the papers. Finding them, I handed them to him without looking while I dug through my purse for my license.

"This is expired." I couldn't say his voice was happy, but I could definitely sense a certain amount of satisfaction behind his words.

"What?" Of course, the registration was expired —why wouldn't it be? The battery had been disconnected; the car hadn't been driven in a long, long time. Why hadn't I thought to check the registration? But then, who was I kidding? Even if I'd known, I'd have taken the risk and driven it, anyway. I had to be on that bus. Had to be.

"Step out of the car, please, ma'am." He opened the door and held it open. With a grimace, I did as instructed.

"Look, Sheriff, I apologize. I didn't think to check

the registration. My bad. The thing is, I've got a ticket on the eight o'clock bus. My phone died, Grandma's phone is disconnected, and I had no way of calling a cab. Using her car is my last resort to catching that bus."

"It's the driver's responsibility to check the vehicle they are in control of has the appropriate and valid registration." He sounded like a robot, and I ground my back teeth but remained silent.

"It's also the driver's responsibility to make sure the vehicle is road-worthy before getting behind the wheel."

"Of course it is." Refusing to look at him, I gazed off into the distance. Could I walk it from here? I could see the silhouette of Maxxan on the horizon. It would take at least twenty minutes if I started walking now.

"What's the time?" I asked.

He glanced at his watch. "Seven forty-five." Damn it. Not enough time to walk it. A jog might cut it. Unless I could convince the sheriff to give me a lift.

"Sheriff, I *need* to get on that bus."

"You'll be on your way soon enough." Pulling out a notepad, he slowly circled Grandma's car, making notes. I waited. It crossed my mind that I could steal his truck, for it sat parked behind me, lights still flashing, engine running.

"I wouldn't," he murmured, still writing.

"Sheriff, you've made it pretty clear you'd like me out of this town. I would have thought at this point in time you'd see yourself clear to helping me. The longer you delay me here, the more likely it is that I'm going to miss that bus—and I've gotta be honest. I don't have the money for another ticket. I miss that bus, and I'm stuck here—and you're stuck with me."

"This vehicle is unroadworthy. Look at those tires! It's not safe."

"So fine me and get it over with."

"Oh, I intend to. Driving an unroadworthy vehicle, driving an unregistered vehicle, the charges are stacking up. And you've just admitted you don't have the funds to pay the fine."

"I've got thirty days to pay, don't I?" I challenged, chin up, despite the sense of doom settling over me. With each second that ticked away, I knew the chances of catching the bus were slimmer and slimmer. My skin was prickling. Sweat was trickling down my back and not just from the heat, but my own anger. Things weren't going my way, and I wasn't happy about it. A zap of static electricity puffed the dust at my feet.

"What was that?" The sheriff looked at my boots, then back at my face, frowning.

"What was what?" We eyeballed each other for several long seconds before he blinked and began walking to his truck.

"Am I free to go?" I asked hopefully.

"Hardly. I need to run your license through the system. Wait there."

Frustration bubbled through me. I didn't want to be here, in a town where everyone hated me, where I wasn't liked or wanted. I longed for the freezing temperatures of Fairbanks, where I had a handful of almost-friends and a job that, while it didn't make me rich, paid the bills.

Throwing up my hands, I moved to the front of Grandma's car and leaned against the hood, arms crossed over my chest. My simple plan of getting to the bus depot had gone horribly pear-shaped, and if I missed the bus, I was all out of luck—I had a non-refundable ticket. Then it hit me. Aunt Martha had given me a wad of cash yesterday for this very purpose! I practically fist-pumped the air. Crisis averted. Yes, I'd lose out on a big chunk of money, but all was not lost in the whole scheme of things. I could grab a ticket for the next bus—and this time, I'd camp at the bus depot if I had to.

"All clean, Shelton. Surprisingly." The sheriff handed back my license, along with the fine for driving unroadworthy and unregistered.

"Twelve hundred dollars?" I shrieked, reading the numbers in his messy handwriting.

"You broke the law. That's the price you have to pay. If you can't pay, thirty days in jail will suffice."

"Never." Oh, how I wished I could see his eyes right now, so I'd know if he was taking pleasure in punishing me like this. But his eyes were hidden behind his sunglasses, and all I could see was myself reflected in them.

"Can I go *now*?" I asked, stuffing the slip of paper into my back pocket.

The sheriff glanced at his watch. "You've missed your bus."

"No shit. I'll get the next one."

"You just said you couldn't afford another ticket," he pointed out.

"I just remembered my Aunt Martha spotted me cash for a ticket. I'm good."

"No. You're not." He shook his head, looking smug.

"What have you done?" My voice dropped at

least three octaves, coming out more of a growl. The cocky expression on his face told me I wasn't going to like what he had to say next.

"Given that you have a criminal record, you can't leave Maxxan until those fines are paid."

"That's ridiculous. You're making that shit up. I would have thought you'd be pleased to see the back of me, but with all these charges, why Sheriff, a girl could be fooled into thinking you wanted her to stay."

He opened his mouth to respond when a black SUV pulled up next to us. The sheriff shut his mouth without uttering a word.

"Need some help here?" SIA Agent Jordan Buchanan wound down his window and rested his arm on it, glancing from me to the sheriff and back again.

"Had a tip-off that someone was out here driving an unregistered and unroadworthy vehicle. Decided to check it out," the sheriff told him, tipping his hat ever so slightly.

"You were tipped off?" I was appalled.

I held up my hand, cutting him off. "No. I don't want to hear it. Whatever it is you think you have to say, Sheriff. You've done your duty here today. I'm sure the people of Maxxan are incredibly grateful that you've prevented my sorry ass from leaving town." The shock had worn off, and now my anger was climbing high and fast. I could feel it thrumming through my veins, heating my skin. The flush on my cheeks wasn't from the sun, and another shot of static electricity shot from my fingertips, puffing the dust at my feet. I had to get out of here before I zapped the sheriff with something more potent than static electricity.

Spinning on my heel, I wrenched open the passenger door and retrieved my backpack, leaving my coat where it lay. Wouldn't be needing it anytime soon, by the looks of things.

"Want a lift?" Agent Buchanan called to my retreating back.

"Nope." I couldn't be around anyone for fear my demon would break loose, and then they'd all regret forcing me to stay. It was clear some sort of conspiracy was afoot; I just didn't know what, and I wasn't in the right frame of mind to find out.

I heard a car door slam and footsteps jogging my way. "Were you following me?" It seemed highly suspicious that he showed up when he did.

"I was driving by," he replied, matching his strides to mine.

"Well, if you wanted a date…" Again, sarcasm came to the rescue.

"I don't."

"Ouch."

"But I might be the one person that can help you."

"Help me? Thought you wanted me to help you?"

"Both. Mutual assistance."

"You don't know me, Agent Buchanan. Ask the locals. They'll tell you."

"That you're crazy? Mental? Insane?"

"You forgot crazy good in bed." I stopped and faced him. "What do you want from me?"

"I want someone who knows the area, the people. I want you on my team."

I laughed. "You must be desperate!"

"The situation's desperate."

"And what exactly is the situation?"

"Deaths. Three so far. Officially…coyotes. Unofficially? Vampires."

"I don't do well with authority or taking orders." I didn't want to think about vampires, didn't want to remember. "These days, I barely do sober."

"Then I'll just ask your brothers. Or one of your cousins."

"Leave them out of this."

"Clearly, I'm talking to the wrong Shelton. My boss considers what's happening here in Maxxan as urgent, and they will do whatever it takes to resolve the situation."

"Good for them. Don't follow me again. I don't like surprises."

Standing in front of the refrigerator later that day, I surveyed the contents. A handful of leftovers from the wake. Two beers. Grabbing one, I popped the top and took a long swig.

"How are you going to get yourself out of this one, Shelton?" I asked out loud. As if in answer, I heard the sound of a vehicle pulling up outside. Throwing open the front door, I stood and watched as Cam climbed down from the cab of his truck. Another vehicle pulled in behind him, and Tyler climbed out.

"You got more of them?" Tyler called, indicating my beer.

"Nope. I got nothing." I smirked, taking a swig.

"Good thing I brought these, then." With a grin, Tyler heaved a carton of beer onto his shoulder and grabbed a grocery bag with his free hand. "Out of the way, girl. Cam, grab the rest, will you?"

I watched, surprised, as my brothers carried groceries—and beer—into the house. I'd been about to follow them in when another vehicle rolled up. Paige and Cody climbed out, both of them carrying bags.

"What's going on?"

"We're here to help." Paige winked as she pushed past.

"Come on, we'll explain inside." Cody bounced up and slung an arm around my shoulder, guiding me into the kitchen. I wasn't quick enough to catch the keys Tyler threw at me. They hit my chest and bounced to the floor.

"Ty!" Paige reprimanded him. "No throwing in Grandma's house." She bent and picked up the keys, holding them out to me.

"What's this? What's going on?" I looked around the room at my cousins suspiciously.

"These,"—Paige jiggled the car keys—"are for you. They are the keys to the spare truck from Cam's garage. So you have a set of wheels to get you around. And these,"—she nodded at the three large garbage bags sitting on the dining table—"are clothes. I raided my wardrobe, and Katie had some stuff she left behind."

"Guys! You didn't have to do this."

"Pft." Cody squeezed my shoulder. "Look, I know yesterday blindsided you, Grandma leaving you the house and all the conditions attached to it. And the less than welcoming reception you got from some. But we want you to know from us firsthand that we want you to stay. And it's not just about the house. We're family. Grandma was right, one hundred percent—the olds should have had your back. They didn't, and while we can't right that particular wrong, we can be here for you now and, well…" He shuffled from foot to foot. "We just want you to know that."

"Fuck," I choked, eyes welling, emotion clogging my throat.

"We also know you're not used to this,"—Cam waved his arm, indicating them all—"and it's probably as overwhelming as hell, so let's go fire up the grill and cook some steaks. You did get steaks, didn't you, Ty?"

My two brothers immediately started bickering and roughhousing, easing the tension.

"Mom told me she gave you money for a bus

ticket." Travis had arrived and helped carry the bags of clothing upstairs to my room while the others gathered in the kitchen to prepare dinner.

"I'll give it back," I replied immediately.

"Don't be stupid. It's yours. Do what you want with it. I just wanted to apologize. It was a shitty thing for her to do, and I'm sorry."

"No need." I shrugged.

"There's every need, Rae. You deserve better." He wrapped me in a hug, and I swallowed back the tears again. I hadn't been expecting this, this love and support from my family. They were getting under my guard and making me feel again. I wasn't sure I liked it. The more you cared, the more it hurt when it was taken away.

Dinner was loud, funny, and delicious, and a brilliant distraction after the events of the day. After I'd walked back to Grandma's, I'd taken a dip in the pond half a mile from the back of the house. I'd splashed around for a bit and then floated and now sported a sunburn for my trouble. But I'd felt better, and that was the most important thing. My anger had been so intense I feared I'd start a wildfire. Dowsing off in the pond had seemed the logical thing to do.

"So, what's the plan?" Paige asked after we'd finished eating and had cleared away the dishes.

"Find a job," I said. Sounded easy. I knew it wouldn't be. My reputation preceded me. Who'd hire the mentally unstable Rae Shelton?

"You're a bartender in Fairbanks, right?" Cody asked. I nodded. "Plenty of pubs in Maxxan. You should pick something up."

"Depends if they know me or not. I have a reputation here. Not a good one."

"It's illegal to discriminate," Paige argued.

"Yeah, but I have a criminal record," I pointed out.

"You didn't go to jail, though. Doesn't that count for something?"

"I went to an asylum for the mentally deranged. Which one sounds better?"

The silence that fell was unnerving, even to me. Who could ever forget I'd been locked away, labeled criminally insane? Not only for my rebellious actions, but also because of my talk of vampires, for I refused to change my story of how Grandpa died. Vampires killed him. No one believed me. Ever.

"I'm sorry that happened to you," Paige whispered.

"Me too." I shrugged off their pity. I didn't need

it. It didn't change anything. I'd done the things I'd been accused of doing. I'd accepted my punishment as my due. I didn't want to revisit the past—the three long years I'd spent locked away for my crimes, the things that had happened to me behind those locked doors. It was the stuff of nightmares, and the less my family knew, the better.

It felt surreal living in Grandma's house. And claustrophobic, even though the place was huge. Everywhere I turned were reminders of her and Grandpa. I'd opened the door to her bedroom and had to close it again—the scent of her in the air had almost crippled me. So, when Mom called saying she and my aunts were coming to sort through things and clear out Grandma's belongings, I felt a rare moment of euphoria. I was trapped in this town for now, but if I could make this house my home, even temporarily, it would give me some reprieve from my own tormented thoughts. I hoped.

Surprisingly, my demon had remained relatively docile, despite the couple of bouts of static electricity shooting from my fingertips. I hadn't had any other outbreaks, and for that, I was thankful. I also knew it was only a matter of time—I'd erupt sooner or later, and I shuddered to think what would happen when I did. Last time I'd been a teenager, young, weak. Now I was an adult, and I could feel my demon. It was so much stronger in me now, more than it had ever been.

All three women arrived at the same time. I took it as my cue to leave. Grabbing the keys to the truck, I stood aside, holding the front door open for the women to enter.

"You're not staying?" Mom asked, a flash of disappointment crossing her face before she hid it behind a smile.

I shook my head. "Gotta find a job, Mom. I'm sure you've all heard what happened yesterday."

"We did. I'm sorry."

"Not your fault, and I don't need you apologizing for me." My words came out harsher than I intended, and I winced. "Look, Mom, I've gotta run. Thanks for taking care of Grandma's stuff. I couldn't face it."

Spinning on my heel, I vaulted down the front steps and through the gate to where my truck waited. It was red, faded, a little dented in places, but I didn't care. It was a set of wheels, and that's all

I needed. As I drove off, I contemplated the idea of driving back to Alaska. Would the truck make it? It was driving fine now, but would it hold up on such a long journey?

There were three bars in Maxxan, and I pulled up in front of the first one I came to, The Looking Glass. It was modern, with lots of glass and mirrors. I knew I didn't fit in as soon as I stepped inside in my jeans, boots, and tank. Heads turned in my direction and a hush settled over the few people who were seated at a nearby table. I was about to chastise them for drinking this early in the day when I noticed the coffee cups in front of them on saucers. This was so not my vibe. Regardless, I approached the bar and bit my tongue while the bartender gave me the once-over with a disapproving arched brow.

"Think you've wandered into the wrong place." She sneered, "Stanley's is that way." She nodded toward the door I'd just come through.

"Any jobs going?" Ignoring her suggestion, I slid onto a barstool and planted my elbows on the bar.

"No. And we have a rigorous hiring process."

"Meaning I wouldn't pass."

She shrugged and continued whatever it was she was fussing with behind the counter. Then I caught a glimpse in the mirror behind her. A gun. She'd pulled a pistol from wherever she'd had it hidden, and it was now lying on top of a tray of glasses, her hand resting on top of it.

"I assume you know who I am?" I asked, slowly rising, not wanting to spook her and have her blow a hole in me.

"You're the crazy Shelton girl."

"Rae. Rae Shelton," I corrected.

"You went to school with my brother."

Oh boy. This should be good.

"Oh?" She'd have to remind me because I had no idea who she was, let alone her brother.

"Paul Baldell." She looked at me expectantly, and I looked back, none the wiser. The name didn't ring a bell, but that wasn't surprising since my memory had more holes than Swiss cheese, thanks to the Institute.

"Seriously?" she squeaked, clearly growing agitated. "You don't remember burying his bike in a load of manure?"

I cocked my head, thinking. A vague recollection surfaced of stealing the Sullivans' tractor and scooping up a bucket load of horseshit. I don't remember what I did with it, but it sounded feasible that I'd empty it all over someone's bike.

"Are we talking bicycle or motorbike?" I asked.

"Motorbike!" she practically shouted. Time to go. Her fingers had wrapped around the handle of the gun, and I knew now was not the time to tell her I had zero recollection of that event. Clearly, she did, and it had made an impact on her brother, too, I assumed. I made a mental note to try to find out what her brother looked like so I could avoid him. It was not going to be easy being back in Maxxan.

"Pass on my apologies to your brother." I tossed the words over my shoulder as I headed towards the door. She wouldn't shoot me in the back. I hoped. Shit, she probably wouldn't shoot me at all. Too scared of getting her prissy ass thrown in jail, but you never know; people do unexpected things under pressure.

My morning followed the same pattern. People recognized me on the street and either crossed the road to avoid me or hurled insults at me. The second bar had no vacancies but told me I could leave my details, and they'd get in touch. I doubted that they would, but I filled out the form anyway and left with a smile that made my face ache.

The third bar was on the outskirts of town. The paint was peeling, and the windows were filthy. The parking lot wasn't paved, and I dodged the potholes as my truck bounced to a stop. Welcome to Stanley's.

Pushing through the doors, I breathed in the smell of stale beer and old smoke. This place was ancient, and it looked like a strong wind would blow it over, but there were no fancy coffee cups on the tables and no massive coffee machine behind the counter. Just beer taps and bottles of alcohol on the shelves.

"What can I get ya?" A grizzly old man shuffled along the bar. Drying a glass, he drew level and eyeballed me. "You here to cause trouble?" he asked, leaning forward and getting in my face.

I shook my head. "Nope. Looking for a job, actually."

"Is that so?" He leaned back, cocking his head. "Got any experience?"

"Five years in a bar back in Fairbanks."

"So, if I rang and asked about ya, they'd give ya a good rap?"

"Good question," I replied. "But yeah, I think so." I'd called my boss the night before, had explained that I was stuck in Maxxan for the foreseeable future. He hadn't cared one way or the other, which had been a blow to my ego since I'd been working for him for the last five years and managing his bar for the last two.

"You going to be trouble?" the old man asked, rubbing the glass so hard I feared it would shatter beneath his hands.

"Can't promise anything, but it's not my intention. I'm guessing you know who I am."

"Girl, you are notorious around these parts. At least you have been recently. Ever since the townsfolk heard you were coming back for the funeral, they've been all up in arms, fearing the worst."

"Was I really that bad?"

"Truth be told, some of them stories may have been vastly exaggerated." The old man grinned. "But I like a girl with spirit. I'll give ya a shot."

Holding out his hand, he said, "I'm Stan." Accepting the handshake, I smiled at Stan, the proud owner of Stanley's.

"Thank you. You won't regret it," I promised.

He laughed. "I think I will, but it will be interesting to see, won't it? You just might liven this joint up a bit."

Word must have spread because when I returned for my shift that evening, the place was packed. After the fourth person wanting to take a selfie with me, I was over it. So was my demon by the feel of things, and I felt a twinge of unease. Everyone was gawking at me like I was a goddamn tourist attraction. I even had a young woman ask for my autograph.

Grinding my teeth, I closed my eyes, trying to calm myself. The last thing I needed was to prove all these assholes right—that I was still as crazy as ever.

"When you've finished daydreaming, Shelton, I'll have a beer." The unmistakable voice of Agent Buchanan reached my ears, and my eyes sprang open.

"Didn't think this place was your style, Agent."

"Heard a buzz about town that this was the place to be tonight. Thought I'd check it out." His grin told me he was enjoying my discomfort.

Pouring him a beer, I placed it in front of him without a word. I had a plan. Get through this shift, don't lose my shit. Eventually, the fuss would die down, people would get tired of waiting for me to explode, and I'd become yesterday's news. Just stay calm, stay under the radar, and keep the demon at bay.

And it was going well. It was working. Hours into my shift, and the crowd had thinned out.

They'd seen what they came to see—me—and found me lacking. I was merely a girl, working behind a bar. So what? No big deal. I ignored the agent who'd set up camp at the far end of the bar. He'd had two beers and then switched to soda. Not that I was keeping tabs on him.

I was walking around collecting empties and wiping down tables when it happened. A strong male arm wrapped around my waist and pulled me backward into him, thrusting suggestively against my ass and breathing into my ear, "How about some sugar?"

My reaction was immediate and reflexive. Grabbing his wrist, I tossed him over my shoulder and slammed him into the ground. His breath wheezed out as his lungs contracted from the impact. I didn't help his breathing any by straddling him and beating the ever-living shit out of him. My demon was roaring inside, happy with the violence and wanting more, more blood, more pain.

I was wrenched off of the now-unconscious man, kicking and yelling. Someone had a death grip around my waist and was dragging me outside while I writhed and twisted in his grasp, throwing my head back to try to head-butt him, kicking my legs, anything to inflict pain.

"Calm down!" Slamming me against the side of the bar, rough hands gripped my shoulders, and the dark eyes of SIA Agent Jordan Buchanan bore into mine. I continued to struggle and didn't still until his fingers wrapped around my throat and squeezed. Not enough to kill, but enough to cut off my airway and get my attention.

"Calm," he ordered, loosening his grip when I finally stopped thrashing about. "Take a breath."

I did. I dragged in a deep, gulping breath of night air. Then another. And another. My mind was whirling. What had just happened? What had I done? My demon hadn't fully emerged, but it was there, just beneath the surface, wanting more, my control of it fragile.

With my eyes locked on Buchanan's, I continued to breathe, focusing on nothing more than dragging air into my lungs. I dimly registered that the knuckles on both of my hands were throbbing. I didn't dare look. What had I done to that man?

"Is he?" It was barely a whisper, but Buchanan heard. His hand was resting on my throat, not hurting, but prepared, not willing to release me just yet.

"He'll be okay. He's probably had worse, though never from a girl." His casual shrug disarmed me. I'd just beaten a man to a pulp. Why wasn't he...mad? Why wasn't he arresting me?

"You want me to?" He cocked his head, one dark brow arched. I shook my head. How was it that he knew what I was thinking?

"It's a talent."

"Stop!" I gasped. My brain was a whirlwind of confusion. The inner battle to subdue my demon had exhausted me, and I closed my eyes, letting my head thump back against the wall.

"Are you hurt?" he asked now, his voice laced with concern, his hand moving from my throat to my shoulders. I shivered.

"As if," I growled, dragging open my eyes, hating myself for showing him weakness. Straightening up, I moved away, telling myself I wasn't disappointed when he let his hands drop from my body.

"What happens next?" I asked. There had to be repercussions for what I'd done. There always had been in the past, only now, I had a feeling the price was going to be even higher. The question was—could I afford to pay?

"I've got a proposition for you," he said, watching me carefully.

I didn't wait for him to finish. He was no better than the asshole in the bar; only he was prepared to blackmail me to get me in the sack. I lost what little control I had and was on him in an instant. We went down with a thump and a cloud of dust. I wasn't entirely sure where he ended, and I began; our limbs were tangled, and my fists were flying, his too, judging by the throbbing in my jaw. Yet I felt no pain; my body was humming again, the energy building, electricity zapped from my fingertips, and I heard him curse.

"Calm. The fuck. Down," he gritted, getting the upper hand and pinning me to the ground on my stomach, my face pressing into the dirt. It didn't work, of course. I just bucked and fought that much harder. We were rolling across the parking lot, grunts and curse words flying, me leaking electricity while one small fragment of my mind tried to rein in my demon, stop it from setting him and the bar on fire. As if sensing my weakness, my demon seized control for one split second, and a fireball shot from my hand, igniting a car in the lot.

Then the world stopped. Everything stopped. My breath. My heart. Silence. His mouth was on mine, his lips hot as they pressed against mine. I was stunned. My demon froze, caught unawares. And just like that, Buchanan had control. And he wielded it well. One big hand cradled my jaw, angled my head, and his mouth plundered mine while I was helpless to resist. I opened to him, and he stormed my mouth, his tongue brushing and stroking, teasing me. I gladly joined in; my hips involuntarily arched against him where we lay on the ground. Slowly, he ended the kiss and raised his head.

"Do you have control now?" he asked, voice rough. I nodded. My demon had subsided with barely a whimper. Only now reality was starting to trickle in, and I could hear the crackle and rumble of a fire burning nearby.

"What did I do?" The horror in my voice was unmistakable. I blinked, looking beyond him and up into the night sky. This couldn't be happening again. It couldn't.

"Follow my lead." His mouth was at my ear, sending a delicious shiver through me, but I was confused. What did he mean? Then his mouth moved down my neck, his lips sliding across my skin, and I arched beneath him. Vaguely, I heard voices and realized the folks in the bar had rushed outside to investigate the fire. Then I heard their snickers and laughter as they spotted us rolling around in the dirt. Oh great. I stiffened beneath him, and he lifted his head again, watching me with analytical eyes.

"I need you to keep quiet and keep it together. Can you do that?" he asked. I nodded. Lifting himself off me, he held out a hand and hauled me to my feet. I brushed myself off, refusing to meet his gaze.

"What's going on out here?" Stan asked, pushing through the crowd, eyeing Buchanan and me before he spotted the car well and truly ablaze. "What in the tarnation? I hope one of you knuckleheads has called the fire brigade."

There was a flurry of activity, patrons retrieving fire extinguishers from their trucks, cell phones out, filming the blaze, and others on the phone to the authorities. Agent Buchanan taking control. I shuffled back into the shadows, leaned against the wall with my arms over my chest, and watched. It was only a matter of time. Surely Buchanan had called the sheriff, arranging my arrest for arson. It wouldn't be the first time.

Apparently, I wasn't the only one who felt that way. I heard them talking, speculating that wasn't it interesting how I was back in town, and now a car mysteriously caught fire in the parking lot of the bar where I worked. I had a feeling "worked" was in the past tense, for Stan approached me now, his face a cross between anger and sadness.

"Rae, Agent Buchanan tells me it looks like a fuel leak, and someone tossed a cigarette butt, and whoosh, it all went up in flames. Care to tell me different?"

I thought for a moment, confused as to why Buchanan was covering for me. We both knew I shot a fireball during our tussle and that I lit the fire, whether intentionally or not. But could I risk telling the truth? With my record, they wouldn't ask twice. I'd be in jail, or worse, back in the institute before I could blink. Reluctantly, I shook my head.

"I will take yer word for it. You've got enough on yer plate to deal with."

"Oh?"

"Small matter of you assaulting a patron? Knocked him clean out, you did."

"Fuck." I'd forgotten. In all the fuss about the fire, I'd forgotten the man I'd beaten the shit out of inside. "I guess I should apologize?"

Stan lifted one shoulder in a shrug. "Up to you. From what I saw, he deserved it. But Rae, girl, I can't have my barkeeper beating down on people."

"I didn't get the job." Didn't take a genius to figure it out. I couldn't blame Stan. I wouldn't hire me either, not after that little display. Even though his takings this evening were probably the best in years, fights and fires weren't good for business.

"You didn't get the job. But I will pay you for your shift tonight." At least he wasn't a total asshole about it, and I appreciated being paid. "Come on to the office, and I'll get that sorted for ya. Cash okay?" He winked, and I grinned, following him inside. Cash was perfect. I didn't let myself think about the fact that I'd just blown my last chance at paid employment.

EIGHT

I drove home with the headlights of Agent Buchanan's SUV in my rearview mirror. I still couldn't figure out why he'd covered for me, and I was starting to think I'd jumped the gun on his proposition. Maybe, just maybe, I should have heard him out before punching him in the face. Now that I'd calmed down, I realized that the agent probably didn't need to proposition women to get them into bed. I was pretty sure with the way he kissed, he'd have them falling all over themselves to join him between the sheets. Which meant he had a totally different proposition in mind, and I needed to drag my mind out of the gutter.

He pulled up beside me when I arrived home, and we both slammed our doors in unison. For some reason, that tickled my funny bone, and I couldn't contain the grin that curled my lips—until I saw his face, and the smile was wiped from mine.

"You're angry." It was a statement, not a question, as I studied him under the glow of the moonlight.

"Nope." He folded his arms over his chest, and I peered at him. Had I misjudged his mood? I didn't think so. He looked pissed to me.

"Tell me about this proposition and then get out of my hair." I was on the defensive. My night had been ruined, and I had no one to blame but myself. That rankled more than pissing in my own bed.

"Join the SIA, and I'll teach you how to control your demon."

"You still want me on your team?"

He nodded. "Yes."

"Why?"

"Because you have the skills that I need."

"Ha!" I scoffed. "I have no skills beyond how to pour a decent beer. Somehow, I don't think the SIA would think that would be very beneficial."

"You're not even aware of what you're capable of," he said, shaking his head.

"Enlighten me then." I was tired, physically and emotionally. My calm, uneventful life had been torn apart, and I craved to return to my peaceful existence in Alaska.

"Join the SIA," he responded, deadpan. Was this his game plan? Refuse to tell me anything until I agree to join his stupid agency?

"You're a dick." Blue electricity danced across my fingertips, and I quickly clenched my hands into fists. Not fast enough for Buchanan, who reached out and grabbed my hand, holding it firmly in his. I ignored the tingle of an entirely different kind that sparked from where his skin touched mine. I had a feeling he was going to be a distraction I was going to regret.

"See this?" He uncurled my fingers and cradled my palm in his. "You can control this."

"But I can't," I protested, trying to pull my hand away, but he held firm. "It builds up, and I have no control over it at all. It takes over, my demon takes over, and bad things happen. Real bad things. If you keep pushing me on this, it's going to happen again, and it's going to be your ass that gets singed."

"So mouthy." He shook his head with a sigh. "I can help you, Rae. Trust me."

Trust him. As if it were that simple. I tilted my head and studied him, unable to read his expression in the dim light.

"You know nothing about me." Of that, I was confident. Until his next words had my heart hitting my toes. "Oh, I know all about you. I know you better than you know yourself—and that should scare you. I've got access to all of your files, Rae. All of them. Your police record. Your patient files at the Institute. Your SIA file. I know your life story. I know every. Little. Thing. About. You." He punctuated the last words with a poke in my chest as if trying to drive home his point.

"Now you're being an asshole," I grumbled, tugging my hand from his and stepping back. The bastard was right. Now I was scared. How could he know all that he claimed?

He shrugged. "It doesn't matter what you think of me." Turning his back, he climbed the front steps and deftly retrieved the spare key from its hiding spot, unlocked the door, and held it open for me.

Stomping my feet like a three-year-old, I pounded past him, annoyed that I was on the back foot with him, that he knew things I didn't, that he learned things about me that I'd forgotten.

Flicking on the living room light, I stood frozen for a moment, a soft gasp leaving my lips. The family photographs that had dotted the walls and stood on every available surface were all gone. As were the knickknacks that Grandma had gathered over the years. The furniture remained, but it all looked odd without her touch. Empty.

"It appears you've been robbed," he said calmly from behind my left shoulder.

"Only by family." I'd left my mother and aunts in the house this morning. They'd obviously been very thorough with removing Grandma's personal effects. While the house had felt strange before, now it felt just weird. I shivered, headed for the dresser where the whiskey was kept, and sent a prayer of thanks that the women had left it behind. They'd taken the crystal glasses, though. Carrying the bottle into the kitchen, I rummaged in the cupboard and pulled out a glass, pouring myself a generous serve.

"Why should I trust you?" Heaving myself onto the kitchen counter, I took a gulp of whiskey, enjoying the burn, waiting for the heady hit of alcohol to reach my brain.

"Because I'm your best shot at getting out of this town." Hooking a chair with his foot, he flipped it around and straddled it, arms resting across the back.

"Pft," I scoffed. "Tell me something I don't know."

"I know you're a fire demon."

"That isn't something I don't know. It's interesting that you know it, but since you say you're with this fancy pants SIA getup, I guess I'd expect you to know that. Why haven't we heard of you before? Why are you turning up now?"

"So many questions." He chuckled, and my annoyance grew.

"How about some answers? Or is this all bullshit? Are you playing some sort of game? Some sort of payback for something I've done to you or yours in the past?" My list of people with grievances against me was long, and just because I didn't recognize him—or his name—didn't mean I hadn't done wrong by him in the past. It was such a pain in the ass when karma catches up with you. I took another mouthful of whiskey.

"No games. I am with the SIA. I do need your help, and I do want you to join my team."

"I don't understand why," I said and then mimed zipping my lips shut when he quirked a brow at me.

"I've already told you. You don't get more until you're on the team."

"So, this is blackmail?"

He shrugged. "Call it what you want."

"I haven't heard of any mysterious deaths in Maxxan. Did hear we have a problem with an overpopulation of coyotes, though?" I still couldn't believe what he'd been telling me, that Maxxan had a vampire problem. I'd held firm to my vampire beliefs for so long, with no one believing me, that now that he was telling me vampires did exist and were creating havoc in Maxxan, I had trouble believing him.

"I'll show you." I watched as he stood, pulled his phone from his back pocket, swiped over the screen, and then headed toward me. His long-legged stride sure was mesmerizing, and I found I couldn't drag my eyes from his corded thighs encased in denim.

"Eyes up here, Shelton."

He wiggled the phone, and I dragged my eyes to the screen only to shriek, "What the FUCK!" I slapped the phone away, and he only just managed to stop it from flying across the room. I jumped down from the kitchen counter and rounded on him. "What the ever-living fuck was that?"

"Calm down." God. How could he be so emotionless? What he'd shown me was horrific, and my stomach was rolling in protest. A woman, her head torn from her shoulders, blood and gore surrounding her.

"This,"—he held up the phone again, but I refused to look at it—"is the work of a rogue vampire. They turn into rippers, as in, they rip the throat open of their victims."

"Get out," I whispered, pointing to the front door. No more. I couldn't take anymore. Not tonight. Maybe not ever.

He left with a comment about no more whiskey. I heard the front door close softly behind him. Snatching up the whiskey bottle, I cradled it in my arms and cursed him up one side and down the other. The clock ticked on the wall, and I had a vague thought that I should be grateful my mom and aunts hadn't taken that as well. Taking the bottle with me, I climbed the stairs and slid into bed fully clothed, still cradling the whiskey bottle. No more whiskey, my ass. He clearly didn't know me as well as he thought he did.

NINE

E yeing the folded piece of paper that had been shoved under my front door, I figured it was more orders from Buchanan. Join the SIA or else. I snatched it up but took a sip of coffee before flipping it open. It wasn't from Buchanan.

"Holy fucking shit." Pulling my phone from my back pocket, I stared at it for a second, thinking. Who to call? Of course, there was only one person I could call. Buchanan. I put my coffee on the table and patted down my pockets, searching for the card he'd given me—the card that I'd ignored. Now, fingers trembling, I dialed the number. No answer. And no voice mail.

"What the hell, Buchanan!" I yelled at the phone. "Answer me, goddamn it."

Hurrying out to my truck, I kept my phone on my lap and kept hitting redial as I peeled out of the driveway, dust and gravel flying in my wake. They had Tyler. The note had been written in blood. *You for him.* It wasn't until I'd turned it over and realized the note had been written on an old utility bill addressed to Tyler that I realized what it meant. The vampires had him. The note had been written in *his* blood.

"I don't know what's been going on in this shithole town, but they've messed with the wrong Shelton," I growled, speeding out of my driveway and onto the main road. Then I saw it. A black SUV parked by the side of the road. I stopped next to it, engine running, and flung myself out of my truck.

"I called you. You didn't answer. They've taken Tyler."

"I heard." Buchanan climbed out of his vehicle and faced me. "We're monitoring the situation."

"Monitoring the fucking situation? Are you for real? We need to get him back."

"He's already dead."

I punched him. My fingers throbbed from the contact, but I wasn't sorry. It had been instinctive.

How dare he just stand here and say he was monitoring the situation when my brother's life hung in the balance? I did not believe for one second that Tyler was dead. They wanted something. They wanted me. Killing my brother would ensure the opposite.

"Feel better?" he asked sardonically.

"Marginally." I threw the note they'd left me at him, and he scanned it before meeting my eyes.

"Do you know where to find them?"

"I do. Where this whole thing began."

"We need a plan."

Shoving the note into his back pocket, he stood with his hands on his hips, studying the ground as if the answer were written in the soil.

"Well?" I asked, impatient. "We can't afford to stand around here talking."

"Are you prepared to walk in and offer yourself up? What if they don't release your brother? What if they kill you both? What then?"

"Damn it!" I kicked the tire of his SUV. Why was he always right?

"Here. Can you shoot?" He was holding out a gun, a very weird-looking gun. It was silver with a blue glass tube on the top.

"What's that?"

"A pyre gun. It won't kill vampires, but it will incapacitate them for a bit."

I took it from him, felt the weight of it in my hands. It was surprisingly light.

"I'm not that good with guns," I admitted, turning it over in my hands.

"Better get good fast," was his helpful response.

THE VAMPIRES WERE where I'd guessed them to be. The field where they'd attacked Grandpa and me all those years ago. It was the only place that made sense. Yet why here? And in daylight? I'd thought vampires couldn't withstand sunlight, yet here we were midmorning, sun blazing, and the five vampires before me were feeling no ill effects from the sun's rays.

Tyler was tied to a tree. Blood covered his neck and shirt front, but he was conscious. Just. Vampires stood guard on either side of him, while three others milled together in a group several yards away. Lowering the binoculars Buchanan had given me; I assessed my options. Could I hit five vampires with the pyre gun? It was highly doubtful I could hit one. Firearms were not my forte. But what choice did I have? Glancing around, I searched for Buchanan but couldn't see him. I had to trust he was here like he said he'd be.

"Come on out, Shelton," one of the vampires suddenly shouted, making me jump. "We know you're there; we can smell you."

Great. This was going beautifully. Sighing, I stepped out from behind the tree where I'd been hiding, the pyre gun gripped tight in my hand.

"Ahhh, there she is. Rae Shelton herself." He was dressed in black jeans and a white T-shirt, with slicked-back hair. You'd be forgiven for thinking this vampire was James Dean. Hell, maybe he was? His skin was perfectly smooth, not so much as a laugh line to be seen.

"Who are you?" I demanded, buying time.

"Bonno."

"Bonno? What sort of name is that?" I scoffed.

"Don't matter. Now I'd be tossing that gun aside if you value your brother's life," he drawled, cocking his head toward Tyler, who'd raised his head when he heard voices.

"Rae. No. Run." He groaned.

"Shut up, little brother." I held my hands up, with the gun dangling from my fingers. I prayed Buchanan was in place, for it was now or never.

Spinning the gun, I gripped it tight, closed my eyes, and fired. The weapon fired effortlessly, and I hurriedly opened my eyes again in case I accidentally shot Tyler. Turned out I didn't hit anyone, but I continued firing furiously, anyway.

The vamps started to drop, but not from my shots. I had to assume Buchanan was in position and hitting his targets. I was running toward Tyler when I was tackled from the side, arms like steel bands closing around me and driving me to the ground. I heard Tyler screaming my name as I bucked and twisted in the vampire's hold. Bolts of fire shot from my fingers, scorching the earth around us but not finding their intended target.

Then I felt it. The pain of a vampire bite. That same pain I'd felt as a five-year-old girl, one that had never left me. It was like acid being poured into an open wound. As the fangs punctured the skin on my shoulder, I screamed, my whole body tensing, then convulsing. My demon writhed within me, then seemed to grow, sucking up all my energy and then detonating with all the power of a nuclear blast. Electricity and fire erupted, bathing both the vampire lying on top of me, mouth clamped to my shoulder, and myself trapped beneath him.

"Rae!" Tyler's scream reached my ears, and with one last final effort, I managed to pry the vampire loose and wriggle out from beneath him, one hand clamped to my bleeding shoulder. My fire subsided, and, much to my disappointment, the vampire, while smoldering, didn't appear harmed. Although, he was clutching at his throat and spitting on the ground.

Scrambling away, I rushed to Tyler, frantically tugging at the ropes tying him to the tree.

"Run!" I gasped, swaying and holding my shoulder tight. It hurt. A lot. And I felt dizzy and nauseous.

"Rae. Look." Putting his arm around my shoulders, Tyler turned me to look at the vampire on the ground before us. He was now on his back, writhing and clutching at his throat as if choking. His mouth was spewing black tar. Totally gross.

Buchanan approached each vampire he'd taken down and secured them with a glowing collar around their necks and another around their wrists. He came to stand next to us, watching with interest as the vampire twisted and writhed before eventually becoming still, apparently dead.

"Just as I thought," he said.

I whipped my head around so fast I nearly fell

over. "What do you mean? Did you *let* me get bitten?"

"Not intentionally. But you're a lousy shot, Shelton."

"I told you I wasn't good with guns," I grumbled in defense.

"You okay, Tyler? They bite you?" Buchanan tilted Tyler's head to the side to get a better look at the wound on his neck.

"Yeah. Hurt like a bitch, but I'm okay. They didn't do that when they drank my blood, though." He nodded at the dead vampire at our feet.

"I'll call an ambulance. You both need medical attention. I need to deal with this lot. Remember, this was a coyote attack."

"Got it," I said, slinging my arm around Tyler's waist and holding us both up.

"Coyote?" Tyler asked, confused.

"Long story. Just go with it, okay?" I told him, leading him back to the tree he'd been tied to and allowing myself to slide down its trunk until my ass hit the ground.

"How'd they get the jump on you?" I asked, watching as Buchanan dragged the dead vampire away.

"Got me as I was leaving my apartment. They

were on me before I could blink. These bastards are strong, silent, and fast."

We lapsed into silence, lost in our own thoughts, until the ambulance arrived, closely followed by the sheriff.

***

"The sheriff kept me in an interrogation room for hours. HOURS!" I stood in front of Buchanan's desk, hands planted on hips, static electricity making my hair stand on end.

He looked up from the paperwork he was reading with a bored expression. "Hmmm?"

Sliding into the chair opposite him, I planted my elbows on the desk, then winced when it jarred my shoulder. I was sporting a large white dressing over the bite. Buchanan's eyes went to it and then back to me.

"All fixed?"

"Sure."

"You know you heal quickly. No big deal."

"No big deal? It hurt like a son of a bitch—that's a big deal to me! Why are you acting like this?"

"Like what?"

"Like you don't care? That what happened today

doesn't matter. Vampires took my brother. Vampires!"

"Shhh." Pushing his chair back, he walked around the desk and closed the door, leaning back against it to study me. "The public doesn't know what it is I do here."

"What? Right under their nose? In their very own police station?" I scoffed, finding that hard to believe.

"They know I'm a special agent sent to investigate the murders."

"They're murders now? I thought you said they were coyote attacks?"

"We've agreed to go with that as a cover story, but the sheriff is aware something is amiss. He just doesn't know what."

"Like he has blood-sucking night crawlers killing his townsfolk?" That reminded me... "And another thing, how come these vampires were out in the sun? I thought they fried in the daylight."

"So did we. We're looking into it."

"Right." I wasn't convinced he'd turn up much. Something weird was going on in Maxxan, that's for sure.

"What happened? What happened to make me

deserve this? Why are they after me? And they are, aren't they?"

"I can't reveal details of an open case." He pulled out a file and slapped it down on his desk, leaning back in his chair with an air of casualness I couldn't pull off.

"Are you serious?" My voice rose with my eyebrows, which I'm pretty sure had shot into my hairline. "Do they teach douchery at the SIA, or do you have a natural talent?"

"You have an extensive criminal record. You're involved in an assault, not to mention the attack on Tyler." His voice was bland, matter of fact. He had me, the bastard.

"You're blackmailing me? Blackmailing me to help you?"

"You've been attacked by vampires twice and survived. The SIA wants you."

"You'll follow through on your promise?"

"I promised nothing."

"You said you'll teach me how to control my demon."

His smirk told me he knew he had me over a barrel. And I wasn't happy about it.

"Welcome to the SIA, Rae."

"Like it or not, you are now a consultant for the Supernatural Investigation Agency. You need to be smart and discreet, especially when you're hunting vampires."

"Gotcha." Climbing out of Buchanan's SUV, I was about to slam the door when his words stopped me.

"First tip. Conceal your weapon."

"Shit. Right." I tucked the pyre gun into the back of my jeans. Buchanan was still seated behind the wheel, and I frowned at him. "You're not coming with me?"

Apparently, my first *mission* was to identify and detain any vampires within the town limits of Maxxan. Easier said than done now that we knew they were day walkers. They looked like us, blended in.

"I've got every faith in you."

"You do?" That surprised me since even I didn't have a whole lot of faith in myself.

"Just get inside and do your job, okay?" My job was to sniff out any vampires in the nightclub we'd just pulled up in front of. How I was meant to spot them, I didn't have a clue, but Buchanan had seemed confident that I'd know one when I saw one. So far, his training techniques sucked.

"Fine, *Sargent*," I griped under my breath, slamming the door. I crossed the street with long strides. I wasn't dressed for clubbing; that much was blatantly obvious as I pushed through the doors and was greeted with strobe lighting, music so loud my ears wanted to bleed, and young women dressed in obscenely short sparkly dresses. Squaring my shoulders, I nudged my way through the throng, uncaring of my jeans, boots, and customary black tank. My shoulder still sported a dressing, although I was almost healed beneath. Pretty sure I stood out like a dog's balls.

"Watch it." A woman with her hair higher than her IQ snarled at me as I pushed past her. How the hell was I going to spot a vampire amongst all these humans?

"Come here often?" The words breathed in my ear sent a shiver down my spine, and I spun, hand going to the pyre gun in the back of my jeans.

"It *is* you. I thought so." The smile the creep gave me confirmed it. Fangs.

"Hands in the air, bloodsucker, you're under arrest." Whipping out the pyre gun, I aimed it point-blank at his chest. People around me screamed and began stampeding for the exit while the vampire tossed back his blonde head and laughed. Long and loud. What the hell? Didn't he recognize authority when he saw it? *Asshole*.

"The boss is going to love this."

"The boss? Who's the boss?" I demanded; only the vampire laughed again, then leaned his face in close to mine. My demon finally decided to wake up—about time—and blue sparks darted across my skin.

"All in good time. He's not happy that you killed Marko."

"I don't know who Marko is." I flexed my fingers, trying to encourage my power. With the pyre gun and my own strength, I could bring this vamp down. I was sure of it. Of course, I had no way of knowing if that was true or if I could even control my demon once I unleashed it.

"We saw everything on the hill this morning. You don't think we'd have sent Bonno out alone? Careless of him to get his sorry ass captured. We'll spring him later; give him time to learn his lesson first."

I remembered Bonno was the vampire from this morning, the one who had taken Tyler. Only clearly, he wasn't the one behind the whole plan. I needed to find out who the mysterious "boss" was and the best way to do that? Beat it out of the vampire in front of me.

Pulling the trigger on the pyre gun, I smiled when the vampire grunted and grabbed his stomach, but the bastard didn't go down, and I frowned at the gun. Did this thing have different settings? Buchanan had said it was a type of stun gun, to think of it as a Taser on steroids. Well, so far, all it had done was give the vampire a tingling massage of his abdomen. Unfortunately, everyone had seen me pull the trigger, and the club erupted in panic. We were swamped as patrons bolted for the doors, pushing between the vampire and me.

"What part of discreet didn't you understand?" Buchanan grabbed my elbow and dragged me across the street. I'd tumbled out of the doors with everyone else, frantically trying to find the vampire.

"You sent me in there as bait, didn't you?" I had to hand it to him. As underhanded as it was, it was a good idea. I'd have probably done the same.

"What makes you say that?"

"It's what I would have done. I had no way of knowing who was a vampire and who wasn't, but they all know me. Correct?"

"I believe so." He didn't apologize for it, and I kinda respected that.

"You owe me tacos." I headed back toward his car. Our mission was blown for the night. Might as well eat.

"I owe you?"

"If you're going to set me up as bait, the least you could do is buy me dinner."

He whispered something I didn't quite catch, and I grinned to myself. Day one as an SIA Agent may not have gone as planned, but I'd survived and managed to glean some intel to boot. The vampires in Maxxan were an organized crew that had a leader. I had no idea how we would sniff out said leader, but I assumed Buchanan would have a plan.

"I thought you'd have a plan." I scowled, hands on my hips, as I surveyed the firearms laid out in front of me and the targets Buchanan had set up at the back of Grandma's house.

"The plan is you need to learn to shoot—with your eyes open—before you get yourself killed."

"You said you'd teach me how to control my demon. Why can't I use those powers?"

"I *will* teach you, but right now, your powers are too unpredictable. You need backup in the way of a firearm. Tyler told me you were shooting that thing with your eyes closed the entire time." He shook his head in apparent wonder.

"Tyler's a snitch."

"He has your best interests at heart. Now shut up and listen." For the next hour, I did as instructed, which, let's be honest, was pretty rare for me. I had the attention span of a goldfish, or so I'd been told. We all knew I didn't do authority well, so listening attentively and following his directions for an entire hour was somewhat of a record.

"You don't have to jump up and down and cheer each time you hit the target." He sighed for the umpteenth time.

"You take the fun out of everything." I pouted, secretly pleased with my progress, even if he wasn't going to give me any encouragement. I didn't like guns. Never had. My natural inclination was to close my eyes and squeeze the trigger. Today I'd managed to overcome my aversion, and with my eyes open, it wasn't surprising that I managed to hit the target.

We were packing up when Buchanan's cell phone rang. Answering it, he turned his back and walked a few paces away. I couldn't help but admire his butt. When he turned back, I quickly pulled my eyes to his face, a light flush burning my cheeks at getting busted checking him out. Only he hadn't noticed.

"Gotta go. Been another murder."

"Another one? That makes what? Four?"

"Yep." He began packing the variety of guns he'd brought out for training and snapping their cases closed. I helped him carry them to his SUV.

"Get in."

"You're taking me with you?" I was surprised. After last night's fiasco at the nightclub, I thought he may have grounded me.

"You've gotta learn, and this is why I hired you, after all."

"I thought you hired me because you figured out I have something the vampires want."

"That too. Now get in."

We headed toward the opposite side of town, blue and red lights on the dash flashing. My adrenaline was pumping, and I couldn't sit still until he suddenly slammed on the brakes and turned to face me. "Do you need to pee?" he asked.

"What? No!"

"Then, for the love of God, will you sit still? You're wriggling around like god only knows what over there. I don't need the distraction."

"I'm a distraction?" My lips curled in a grin.

"Jesus Christ," he said, returning his attention to the windscreen. We began moving again, and I sat daydreaming about whether distracting Buchanan was a good thing or not. He was hot, no denying it, and the kiss that we'd shared was off the charts. Did I want more? Shit yeah. But now it was complicated. We worked together. I may or may not be stuck in Maxxan for up to a year. And I didn't do relationships. But I did want to jump his bones.

We eventually pulled up at a small house on the outskirts of town. This was what my mom called the wrong side of the tracks. The poor side. Where you did what you could to get by, and your neighbors didn't judge—although they would steal anything of value not tied down.

"Should she be here?" The sheriff greeted us at the bottom of the driveway.

Buchanan dismissed him with a brief, "She's with me." And kept on walking. I followed.

"Oh shit. Fuck." I'd seen bad things before. And this was bad. A woman lay on the patch of dried-out lawn at the rear of the property, her head several feet from her body. But it wasn't the sight so much as the smell. Of blood. Of death. Clapping a hand over my nose, I tried to breathe through my mouth, but you could taste it. I swallowed, trying not to hurl.

"You holding it together?" Buchanan nudged me with his elbow, and I nodded, not wanting to let him down.

"See anything unusual?"

"Other than she's not wearing her head?" I moaned, giving in and turning my back on the body.

"Other than that. Take a look around. Something is up in Maxxan. Vampires walking in the daylight? I work with vampires. Heck, the Director of the SIA is a vampire, and he sure as shit can't tolerate the sun. Whatever or whoever is doing this, it's tied to Maxxan, and it's tied to you."

"Me?" I squeaked, clutching my throat.

"They want you. Why? Biting you kills them,

which leads me to believe it's your blood that is toxic to them. Again, why? Why you?"

"I could ask the same question," I whispered, horrified. He was right. *Wait. He was right?* "Is this why you recruited me? For my blood?"

"Among other things." His shrug was offhand, and I punched him in the shoulder, hard.

"Hey! What was that for?" He flexed his shoulder and rubbed it.

"For being a douche." Stomping away, I began to scan the surroundings, with no clue what I was doing or what I was looking for. It niggled me that maybe, just maybe, I'd been played by SIA Agent Jordan Buchanan. He'd figured out way before me that my blood was toxic to vampires—so, essentially, I could be used as a weapon.

I was at the rear of the property, where the fence had rotted away, when I saw it. Paw prints in the dirt. And not just any paw prints. Mother-fucking massive ones. Bigger than my head. Crouching, I traced it with my fingers, touched the soil, and felt the heat, so hot it almost burned.

"That's not right," I murmured, puzzled. What sort of animal could leave tracks this size, and what kind of animal burned the ground it walked on?

"Find something?" Buchanan crouched next to me, looked at the ground, and back at my face.

"Yeah. These?" I indicated the tracks.

"What? There's nothing there."

"Are you shitting me? Look, douche, it's been a long day. I don't need you pulling my chain, okay?"

"Rae." He wrapped his fingers around my wrist. It was the first time he'd touched me in days, and of course, my heart skipped a happy little beat, and warmth tingled where he touched. I cursed my reaction to him, wanted or not. "I swear I'm not pulling your chain. There's nothing there. Nothing that I can see. Tell me what you see."

"Paw prints. Big paw prints. The ground is charred and hot. You swear you can't see them?"

"I swear. What do you think left them?"

I didn't want to say it, for saying it made it real, and vampires were quite enough for one day, thank you very much.

"Rae?" he prompted.

"Hellhound." My voice was barely a whisper. The vampires had got themselves a hellhound. Heaven help us all.

ELEVEN

"Ouch!"

"Stop being such a baby."

"Stop sticking me with needles then," I grumbled, doing my best not to ogle the muscular chest in front of me. We were in my kitchen, and Buchanan was about to draw my blood. Yes, you heard me correctly. Needless to say, I was not happy about it, but he was right. The answer—or at least part of the answer—was in my blood.

"I haven't even touched you yet. That was just the tourniquet." He was enjoying this, I could tell.

"You know what you're doing, right? You've done this before?"

"We're all trained in basic first-aid and bodily fluid retrieval," he assured me.

"Put that way, it sounds totally gross."

"Ready?" he asked.

I nodded. "No."

His lips curled into a grin, and a dimple appeared on his cheek. I touched it, then quickly snatched my hand away. What was I thinking? Clearly, I wasn't.

"I won't hurt you. Trust me."

Trust him. My heart was pounding. Sweat beaded my skin as he tightened the tourniquet and instructed me to pump my fist.

"You've got good veins." He wiped the inside of my elbow with an alcohol swab.

"Thank you." Panic was starting to set in, and my demon reacted accordingly. Electricity sizzled and zapped in the air, dancing across my skin until I was pretty sure I glowed with it.

"Relax." He hovered over me with the needle poised above my skin, not quite touching.

"I'm relaxed," I lied, another arc of electricity crackling between us.

"Sure you are." He chuckled again, then close to my ear, so close I could feel the warmth of his breath, he whispered, "Close your eyes."

I obeyed.

"Do you want me to kiss you?" My eyes sprang open again.

"What sort of question is that?" A stupid one, I answered silently. Of course, I wanted him to kiss me. My demon stopped zapping and grew intent.

He was so close that it only took the slight movement of his head for his lips to touch mine. I couldn't contain the groan at the contact. My lids fluttered shut, and I basked in the wonder of his kiss. Man, he had skills. The softness of his lips contrasted with the sharp abrasion of his stubble. When his tongue swept along my lower lip, I didn't give a second thought to opening my mouth and consuming him.

The kiss went on and on, and I had zero complaints. Not a one. My heart was racing, but no longer in fear. I was tingling most deliciously, and my demon was practically purring. When he slowly drew away, I groaned in protest, silenced when he laid a finger over my mouth.

"Shh." He stayed close, and I kept my eyes shut. I felt a sharp sting, heard him murmur, "Easy," and then it was done. He moved away. The pressure from the tourniquet was gone, and he was pressing a cotton ball to the inside of my elbow.

"Hold this," he said. How could he be so matter-of-fact when I was sitting here, a red-hot mess of lust and hormones? Was he not affected by our kiss? Then I caught a glimpse of want and need in his eyes, and a smile of pure feminine power curled my lips. It seemed Jordan Buchanan wasn't as unaffected as he liked to make out.

"They're not going to want to bring me in, are they?" I voiced my last remaining fear.

"Who? The SIA? Doubtful."

"I just...don't like being locked away," I admitted, watching as he busied himself with the two vials of blood he'd just taken.

"We're not going to lock you away, Rae, okay? I won't let that happen."

"Then it's a possibility?"

"Jesus, woman. No. It's not. You are in no danger of being locked away by the SIA. As long as you stay on the right side of our laws."

"Which are?"

"Don't go rogue. You start running around burning humans to a crisp, then yes, you are likely to find yourself incarcerated by the SIA."

Before I could reply, Buchanan cupped my chin and studied my face intently.

"Have you been getting *any* sleep?" he asked. I

figured he'd noticed the dark shadows around my eyes.

Lifting one shoulder, I looked into his eyes and tried not to drown. "Not much." I'd been patrolling Cameron and Tyler's neighborhood, making sure they were safe, but they weren't my only family, and I couldn't be everywhere at once. I was terrified one of my cousins would be taken, or my parents, aunts, or uncles. Sleep was a luxury I couldn't afford. Coffee and energy drinks were my new best friends.

"You know vampires cannot enter your home without an invitation?"

"What?" I was tired, confused, and struggling to control my hormones. Not the best combination.

"A vampire cannot enter your home without you inviting it in. So, you are safe at night. You can sleep, as long as you haven't invited any vampires in."

Tyler had been taken as he'd stepped out of his apartment, I remembered. So, we were safe—sort of. We just needed to be vigilant and alert when not in our homes. I yawned, threw open the refrigerator door, and studied the contents. "You're coming back, right?"

"Abandonment issues, Shelton?" he drawled.

"Too tired for your douchery today, Buchanan.

Just hit me with the facts. How long is this going to take?"

"Only a few hours. I've got the chopper booked. You can come too, you know." I was already shaking my head. I'd checked with Curtis Jacobs, the executor of Grandma's will. No leaving town. At all. For one full year. While I wasn't fully committed to this plan of hers, I'd do my best to honor it while I was here. Plus, I wanted to be close to my family in case anything more happened.

"So...I guess..." I continued to study the contents of the refrigerator with unseeing eyes, and he chuckled.

"I'll be back before you know it. Stay out of trouble." I felt the brush of his fingers at the back of my neck, and then he was gone. I remained standing in front of the refrigerator, the cool air swirling around me, cooling my emotions along with my body temperature. Eventually, it beeped at me in outrage, demanding to be closed. I snatched an energy drink from my dwindling supply and dutifully closed the door.

I had a job to do. Pulling out my phone, I synced to the Bluetooth speaker Cam had given me and dialed the volume up loud. "Let's do this bitches!" I yelled over the music. My plan for today was pretty simple. Paint the living room. I couldn't stand to look at the faded outlines where the photographs had once hung, plus if I was going to stay here, I might as well put my mark on the place.

Cam had been a sweetheart and picked up the paint I wanted, a soft shade of gray, and supplied me with paint trays, rollers, brushes, and drop sheets. I was all set to go.

The hours passed quickly, and despite never having painted a room before, I was pleased with the results. The cutting in was a bit rough, but I'd gotten better at it, and by late afternoon the room was done. Exhaustion was pulling at me, making me stumble, and I decided to sit down before I fell down. I'd put the lids back on the paint cans, the brushes and rollers were soaking in a bucket of water on the deck out back, and the whole house reeked of paint fumes.

Lying on the drop cloth, I stretched out, closing my eyes for the briefest of moments. I'll get up and take a shower in a moment, I told myself. Then promptly fell asleep.

When I awoke, it was dark, my music had stopped, and the house was eerily silent. I lay on the hard floor and listened intently. Was someone in here with me? Holding my breath until I saw spots before my eyes, I eventually sucked in a lungful of air and eased to my feet. I convinced myself I was just jumping at shadows when I heard one of the back porch boards creak. Someone was out there. Or something.

Feet bare, I tiptoed across the room and out into the hallway. A shadow crossed the glass of the back door, and I froze, plastering myself to the wall and inching my way toward it. My heart kicked up a notch, and my stomach fluttered, signaling my demon that shit was about to go down. My demon responded appropriately with a brush of electricity across my fingertips. I really needed to nail Buchanan down about teaching me how to control my demon and harness my power.

It crossed my mind that it might not be the wisest thing in the world to confront whoever was sneaking around on my back porch, but since I'd never been one to sit back and think through my actions, there was no point starting now.

I was at the door now and stopped, ear pressed to the wall. Whoever was on the porch had either left or was at the far end. I had two choices. Try to open the door silently and take them by surprise, or burst out and attack, giving them a split-second advantage.

Knowing there was no such thing as opening the back door silently—that mother creaked and groaned like an eighty-year-old with arthritis—I opted for option two. Flinging the door open, I shot out, landing in a fighting stance with my hands outstretched and electricity dancing in my palms.

Of course, no one was there. Deflated, I let my hands drop. Had I just imagined the whole thing? I walked to the edge of the porch and surveyed the back garden and beyond. Crickets chirped, and the moon gave just enough illumination that I wasn't totally blind.

"You're either very brave or very stupid," a voice said from the darkness. I swiveled my head and peered at the talking tree.

"Jury's out," I replied. There. A man stepped away from the trunk of the tree, his shadow separating as he stepped onto the lawn, bathed in moonlight. It wasn't anyone I'd ever seen before, which led me to believe one thing.

"Vampire," I said.

"Smart." He inclined his head. "The boss will be pleased when I return with you." He grinned, and his fangs glinted in the moonlight. My heart leaped, as did the electricity in my palms. As soon as he moved, the electricity turned to flame, and I did my best to concentrate, to use my abilities to my own advantage. I managed to hurl a small fireball at him. He dodged it easily, and then he was upon me. We rolled across the ground, and judging by his grunts, my blows were finding their mark.

He was stronger and faster than me, but I had one thing he didn't. Toxic blood. Only this vampire seemed to know better than to bite me. Flinging me off, he delivered a painful kick to my belly. Groaning, I curled into a ball. Big mistake. He then started kicking my back, and he meant business. Pain and panic flooded through me; my body buzzed as I tried to crawl away. My face was bleeding. Pretty sure half of my internal organs were too. He didn't need to bite me to kill me. He had the strength to beat me to death. The thought was sobering. Not so for my demon, who erupted in what I can only assume was in self-preservation. I was on fire. I was literally a ball of flames, my entire body vibrating so fast my teeth were rattling, and my eyeballs threatened to pop out of my head.

Dragging myself to my feet, I stood and tried to direct some of my fire at the vampire, who'd hurriedly backed away. Buchanan had told me there were two ways to kill a vampire. Decapitation or a stake in the heart. Ripping their heart right out of their chest also worked, he'd added. So, despite my impressive blaze, I knew it wouldn't kill him, but if I could toast him, it would incapacitate him, and maybe, just maybe, I could get some answers out of him. Or kill him. I wasn't fussy about which one occurred.

He must have realized this, too, for he fled. Standing with my hands on my hips, I yelled after him, "Listen up, nutsack, tell your boss that I'm coming for him."

With the danger now gone, I figured my demon would subside. I was somewhat concerned when it didn't. I was still ablaze, from head to toe, and the dry grass at my feet was beginning to ignite. Shit. I spun, checking on Grandma's house, thankful to see I hadn't set it ablaze, but I backed up just in case. The fire trail on the ground followed me. Fuck!

Breathe. Closing my eyes, I focused on dragging a deep breath in through my nose and out through my mouth. Cracking open an eye to check on progress, my shoulders slumped when I was greeted with flame. Was this who I was now? Had it finally happened? This was going to make life really inconvenient if I was a walking, talking fireball.

The blast of water that hit me in the chest caught me by surprise, and I lost my balance, tripping over backward. The water continued, spraying me all over until, eventually, I was doused. My flame was gone, and I was a soggy, dripping mess covered in mud and ash.

"Okay, okay!" I shouted, holding out a hand to ward off the stream from the garden hose.

"You good now?" Buchanan asked, turning off the tap.

"Define good," I griped, struggling to my feet and shaking off as much water as I could. At least I was no longer on fire. I was also buck-naked. My clothes were nothing but wet, burned rags at my feet.

"Tomorrow, we work on controlling your powers," he said, arms crossed, legs planted.

"About time." I stalked past him and into the house, leaving muddy footprints in my wake.

"You okay?"

I swiveled mid-stride and poked him in the chest, "Oh yeah, I'm wonderful if you can call having the ever-living shit beaten out of you by a vampire and then losing control and turning into a human fireball fine. You promised me." I did not like the way my voice wobbled on those last words.

"Are you hurt?" His voice lost some of its usual aloofness, and I tried not to be irritated that he seemed totally oblivious to my naked status. I wasn't sure what I wanted—for him to comment on what a great body I had, or to offer his shirt or what, but it wasn't to be ignored. My female pride stung.

I took a moment to take stock of my injuries. Before I'd erupted in flames, I'd been hurting. Badly. My ribs were broken; pretty sure I'd punctured some things on the inside, but now? Now nothing hurt. I patted myself down, pushed my ribs, touched my face.

"How do I look?" I asked. He arched a brow, his eyes not leaving mine. Okay, so maybe not so oblivious to my nakedness after all.

"Besides wet?" he drawled.

"Haha. Funny. Am I bleeding?"

He peered at my face, then ran his eyes over my body before shaking his head. "Nope." His eyes were back on mine, darker than before.

"I think the fire healed me." This was new. But then, I'd never been a human fireball before. Usually, when I lost control, it was indiscriminately throwing fireballs around, but this time I *was* the fireball.

Buchanan was nodding. "Could be," he said.

"What were the results? Of my blood sample," I demanded.

"Nothing yet. Dropped it off at the lab, and they'll let me know when they're done testing."

"So, what were you doing all day?" I was indignant that he'd left me here to deal with vampires who wanted my ass while he was taking his sweet ass time in Redmeadows doing God only knows what.

"Not that I have to answer to you, *but* I was interrogating the vampires we brought in."

"Oh." Well. That was reasonable. "And?"

"They're not talking. Yet. But we're not done with them. It's early days."

"Right." I nodded.

Grabbing my shoulders, he spun me in the direction of the stairs. "Now go, get cleaned up, and get some sleep. I'll be back at sunrise for your training to begin. Be ready." As I was heading upstairs, I thought I heard him mutter, "Lord almighty." Before the front door shut behind him.

"First of all, you're thinking of your demon as a separate entity, like there are two of you sharing the same body." I was nodding my head, standing in the early morning light, not a scratch or a bruise on me from last night's events. Even the scars from my past had gone. My skin was pristine.

"Are you listening?" Buchanan barked. I jumped.

"Yes. But you're wrong. My demon isn't *me*. It's *in* me."

"Incorrect. This is why you can't control it. Because you believe that you can't. Just like you can't control me. Or anyone else, for that matter. Lift your arm."

I did.

"You did it without even thinking about it, right? It was natural. Automatic."

I nodded.

"That's how it should be with your powers. We're going to stop referring to *it* as your demon because you *are* your demon. You are a fire demon."

"Part fire demon," I corrected.

"Rae." His voice held a warning, and I sighed, "Okay, okay. I'm a fire demon. Rah, rah, rah."

"Do you want me to train you or not?"

I cocked my head, studying him. "What are your qualifications?"

"I'm an SIA Agent."

"No, I mean, to be an SIA Agent, you have to be paranormal. What are you?"

"That's classified."

"Are you serious?" Throwing my hands up in the air, I looked him over. I had no clue what type of paranormal entity he could be.

"Are you a fire demon, too?" I asked. He shook his head.

"Fae?" Again, he shook his head.

"Shifter?" He blinked, and I pounced. "You're a shifter! What sort? Wolf?"

"Why does everyone assume a shifter is a wolf?" He sighed.

"Not a wolf then. Cat?"

"Time to get on with your training."

I gasped, clapping a hand over my mouth. "You're a cat, aren't you?" I jumped up and down with glee. "What sort? A little bitty domestic kitty? Or a jungle cat."

"Rae," he warned, shaking his head.

I laughed out loud. "Oh my God, you're a kitty cat!"

"Do you want me to teach you or not? Because I've got other things I could be doing."

"Okay, okay. Teach on."

Hours. We spent hours outside, but we made progress. I could now summon flame in the palm of my hand with barely a thought. I could mold it, direct it, push it away from me, and pull it back.

The back garden was a patchwork of scorched grass and mud puddles from where Buchanan had put out any spot fires I started. I couldn't be happier. I'd also been mulling over what he'd said. That I didn't have a demon *in* me, but the fact that I *was* a demon. It had been sobering to hear it that way. I'd always thought my demon was a curse, but now I was starting to see the possibilities. I wasn't keen on turning into a human fireball again, but the fact that the fire had healed me? Pretty cool. And now that I was learning to control the flames, well, let's just say I had a cocky swagger to my step when we wrapped up for the day.

TWELVE

"Hey, Mom." I was showered, legs shaved, and dressed in cutoff jeans and a T-shirt sans bra when she rang.

"Hey Rae, your dad asked me to give you a call." When a conversation with your mother started like that, you knew it wasn't going to be good.

"He could have called me himself, you know." I wasn't surprised, though. My dad had taken avoidance to maximum levels since I'd returned to Maxxan.

"I know, sweetheart, but you know how he is. He just..." She blew out a breath. "He just doesn't know how to deal with you."

"He doesn't have to *deal* with me, Mom. Having a conversation is not dealing. It's talking. Jesus."

"I don't want to fight, honey."

"You're right. Sorry. It's not your fault, I know." It was my turn to blow out a breath. Putting the phone on speaker, I balanced it on the bathroom vanity and busied myself, pulling my hair up into a messy knot on top of my head. "So, what does he want?"

"We didn't get a chance to sort through the den when I was over with your aunts, and Dad wanted Grandpa's old books and things. Apparently, there's a lot of family history recorded there somewhere."

"Yeah, that's fine. Did he want to come over and get it?"

"He asked if you could pack the den up and leave the boxes out front. He'll swing by to pick them up."

I was silent for a moment. My father disliked me so much he couldn't stand to see me. It stung. He blamed me for Grandpa's death, and I couldn't fathom how he could hold a grudge for this long. I was his daughter, for God's sake. But we'd had this argument a million times as I was growing up, and each time it pushed us further and further apart.

"Sure," I said instead, masking the hurt.

"We did leave some flat-pack boxes there." Mom couldn't keep the relief from her voice.

"I'll check. I haven't been in there. Haven't been able to bring myself to open the door," I admitted. For while Grandma's bedroom had been all *her,* the den had been all Grandpa.

"I'm sorry to ask you to do this, sweetheart. I'd come and do it myself, but work called and—"

"Mom," I cut her off, "it's okay. You don't have to do it. I appreciate everything you and Aunt Martha and Aunt Sarah have done already. Did Cam tell you I've started decorating?" I changed the subject, filling her in on the paint job I'd done in the living room.

"Cameron also mentioned you have a job. As a deputy?"

"More as a consultant for the SIA. I'd never even heard of them before, have you?"

"I've heard of them, yes, but they've never had a presence here. I wonder if your Agent Buchanan is going to stay on after he's dealt with..." She trailed off, and I wondered how much she actually knew.

"Dealt with the vampires, Mom. You can say it. There are rogue vampires in Maxxan again. Who dealt with them last time, anyway?" I was curious. Grandpa and I had been attacked by rogue vampires. I never did hear what had happened.

"No one dealt with them, honey. After the attack, the vampires simply fled. They've barely had a presence in Maxxan. Only in the last few years have they started to return."

"Weird." Picking up the phone, I headed downstairs and stood outside the den door, staring at the wood grain. "Okay, Mom, gotta go. Thanks for the call. Tell Dad I'll get those boxes packed up. He can pick them up in a couple of days."

"Love you, honey."

"Love you too, Mom." Sliding my phone into my back pocket, I wrapped my fingers around the doorknob and turned.

The den was just as I remembered it. Only dustier. Looked like no one had been in here for quite a while, which was kinda a relief because I couldn't pick up Grandma's scent like I had in her bedroom. The furniture was big, old, and dark. Grandpa's desk stood in front of the window; a leather swivel chair pushed neatly beneath it. One wall was floor-to-ceiling bookcases, crammed with books and random junk. A big old rug covered most of the floor, threadbare in places. By the door was a stack of folded boxes and two rolls of tape sitting on the top.

It had been a long day, and I was tired, but the den wasn't going to pack itself, and the last thing I wanted was a blowout with my father. I figured I'd fill a few boxes tonight and do a few more in the morning, though judging by how many books were jam-packed into the shelves, there was a strong chance I'd need more boxes. And more time.

Crossing the floor multiple times alerted me to it. The squeaky-as-fuck floorboard. Each time I passed behind the sofa, it creaked and groaned. Only passing behind the sofa was imperative if I wanted to get to the bookshelf behind it.

"This is ridiculous." Muttering to myself, I braced against the back of the old Chesterfield and pushed. The damn thing was heavy, but it slid relatively easily thanks to the tattered rug beneath its feet. Of course, the carpet actually moved with the sofa, so now I had a couch in the middle of the room with the rug bunched up against the wall on the opposite side and bare floorboards where the sofa had initially sat. Which was the whole purpose of my exercise.

Standing on the floorboards, I bounced up and down until I found the noisy one, then got down on my hands and knees to examine it. I was more than prepared to go out to the garage and get a hammer and nails if I had to. Only the squeaky floorboard was not just loose. It wasn't secure at all.

"What the hell?" Pulling at the edges, I managed to get a hold and lift the floorboard. "Did you have a hidey-hole, Grandpa?" I reached my hand in and felt around, grinning when my fingers brushed against —what was it? A book? A secret diary, maybe? My imagination ran riot with possibilities, and I pulled the book out. Dust flew into the air, and I closed my eyes on a sneeze. In my hand was a folder, old and brown. The emblem on the front? SIA.

"What? How can this be? I thought the SIA was only formed...when was it? Seventeen years ago?" Putting the file to one side, I reached my hand in again and felt around, but there was nothing else in the hidden space beneath the floorboards. I put the loose board back and wondered what I should do about it, if anything. Deciding the floor could wait, I sat cross-legged, slid the elastic strap off the file, and opened it across my lap.

The pages inside were old and yellow, the words faded but readable. But what I read rocked my world to its very foundations. Grandpa had been involved with the SIA, an undercover agent if you like. And the person he was investigating? His own son. My dad. He believed Dad was involved with a vampire they called the Gunslinger—given the name, I assumed the vamp had been around since the eighteen hundreds, if not longer. There was also mention of the Red Witch that the Gunslinger and the Red Witch were working together.

Did Dad know? Did Dad know Grandpa had been investigating and had records of him? Was that why he wanted the contents of the den, hoping anything Grandpa had squirreled away would be concealed in one of his books for Dad to find? Then my mind took a dark turn. Was Dad responsible for the attack that killed Grandpa? I couldn't get my head around it. Couldn't believe he'd do anything so heinous...and yet?

"Argh!" Shoving the papers back into the file, I carried it upstairs and slid it under my mattress. Changing into jeans, boots, and a fresh T-shirt, this time with a bra, I thumped back down the stairs, snatched up my keys from the hallway table, and headed out. I needed a drink, and I'd consumed all of Grandma's remaining supply.

Twenty minutes later, I bounced across the parking lot at Stanley's, deliberately avoiding looking at the big scorch mark where I'd set fire to a car not too long ago. It already felt like a lifetime had passed since that night.

It was a quiet night. Only a handful of patrons turned their attention to me when I entered.

"At ease, boys," I called out, heading straight for the bar.

"Rae. Good to see ya." Stan shuffled along, dishcloth in hand, wiping down the bar as he went.

"You too, Stan. How's business?"

"Can't complain. What can I getcha?"

"Whiskey. On the rocks."

"Getting classy, eh?" He chuckled, shoveled ice into the bottom of a glass, and poured a generous shot of whiskey over the top. Accepting the golden liquid, I took a sip.

"Ambrosia," I murmured, mostly to myself. Digging around in my back pocket, I pulled out a handful of notes and slapped them on the bar.

"Leave the bottle," I instructed. Snatching up the cash faster than I could give him credit for, Stanley nodded and shuffled to the cash register. How old was he, anyway? A hundred? The lines on his face were deep, and his shuffle indicated mobility was difficult. Yet he'd swiped my money with remarkable speed.

I wasn't sure how long I'd been at the bar, long enough to have a nice buzz going on, when someone slid onto the barstool next to me.

"That seat's taken."

"Oh yeah? By whom?" My head whipped around to discover Buchanan sitting next to me, waving at Stan for a beer.

"Oh, it's you." I turned my attention back to my drink.

"Happy to see you too."

His voice held that slight hint of humor that I liked. It was easy to miss. He kept it hidden well, but if you listened for it, you could hear it—with just a touch, a pinch, really, of sarcasm. It was a talent I admired. Watching him from the corner of my eye, I wondered about my intrepid boss. I'd never met a cat shifter before. Did he shift into cat form for work purposes? It would be a great talent to have during a stakeout. Who'd notice a cat? You certainly wouldn't pay much attention to it. Of course, the downside would be other creatures bigger than you, like dogs. I wondered if he'd ever been chased by a dog. I asked him.

"What? No. I haven't been chased by a dog. Why?"

"Just wondering."

"How many of those have you had?"

"Not enough." Not enough to block out the memory of discovering my grandfather was old SIA, and my father was a bad guy. Potential bad guy, I reminded myself. There was nothing in Grandpa's notes to confirm it. No evidence. Just his suspicions. But they had to be strong to suspect his own son, didn't they?

"What's going on, Rae?" I'd briefly forgotten Buchanan was seated next to me and jumped a little when he spoke. His hand touched mine where it lay on the bar, and that familiar warmth I experienced whenever his skin touched mine did its thing, winding its way through my body, heating me, making my blood sizzle and my body tingle.

"Tell me about yourself, Buchanan." My words were only slightly slurred, and I grinned; the whiskey was working.

"What do you want to know?"

"Oh, I don't know, anything. Something about *you*. You apparently know all about me, but I know nothing about you. Where do you live? Do you have a family? How did you get started in the SIA? Is it what you always wanted to do? Do you have a pack? Where are they?"

Laughing, he held up a hand to cut off my list of questions.

"Okay, okay. First of all, you can stop calling me Buchanan. My name is Jordan."

"Jordan," I dutifully replied, liking the way it sounded on my lips.

"I grew up in Redmeadows. I have an apartment there, but I move around a lot with the SIA. My family is still there. I'm an only child, so it's just my parents. And I don't have a pack, no."

I frowned. "I thought shifters have packs. Cats have packs, don't they? What do they call them? A pride?"

"Pride is for lions."

"So, what then? A litter?"

He laughed. "No, a litter is kittens. Grown domestic cats is a clowder."

"Do you have a clowder?"

"Nope."

"Are you even a domestic cat?" I peered at him, but his face gave nothing away.

"Nope." Hmmm. Not a small cat, then. Maybe he was a jaguar. Or a leopard. Or tiger.

"Do you hack up furballs?" I tilted my head, considering him. "After you shift back, I mean."

He laughed. "No, I do not hack up furballs."

I thought about this for a moment and wondered if he was lying. Would you even bother grooming yourself if you were a shifter cat? In cat form, I mean. I couldn't imagine licking myself clean.

Losing interest in cats, I changed the subject. "Tell me about your family. And the SIA."

"My mom works in administration with the SIA; my dad works in security and is pushing for a seat on the Council. I got involved with the SIA through a buddy of mine, Alex Carter. He convinced me to sign up."

"You like it?" I asked.

"I do."

"You said the SIA has only been in existence for a few years..."

"Officially. I believe they've been around as an underground type of organization for hundreds of years."

"That explains it." I lowered my head, swirling the ice in the bottom of my glass.

"What's going on, Rae? Something's bothering you, I can tell."

"You can tell? You think you know me that well?" I didn't like that he thought that. I was used to being a loner, to not sharing—or caring—with others.

How could he possibly know me from words written in a file?

"You're so feisty." He chuckled, then lapsed into silence, letting it ride, and I cursed him. Because it was what I needed. And he knew it.

"Fine." I finally puffed. "But not here, okay? This place has ears."

"I'll take you home. I'm driving. You've had too much booze." Sliding off the barstool, he led the way, holding the door open for me to pass through ahead of him. I wasn't used to having doors held open for me. It was strange, but oddly pleasant. I hugged the bottle of whiskey I'd swiped from the counter close to my chest. Jordan eyed it, then me. "What?" I said defensively. "I paid for it!"

"She's good," Stan shouted after us, giving a wave.

"See?" I muttered, heading toward his big black nark mobile parked in the lot. Seeing my slightly dented, faded red pickup next to it, I veered toward it instead.

"I said I was driving." Jordan grabbed my elbow, but I wriggled out of his grip.

"You can drive, but we're taking my truck. I'm not being stuck at Grandma's without a vehicle again."

"Oh, but it's okay for me to be stuck there?" He arched a brow, and his head angled just enough that he was the cutest thing I'd seen on two legs all day.

"Totally."

"Fair enough. Keys?" Digging in my back pocket, I pulled out the keys and threw them at him. He caught them easily, and I frowned.

"You haven't had nearly enough to drink," I muttered, climbing into the passenger seat and pulling on my seatbelt.

"You've probably had enough for the two of us."

"Is this going to be a lecture?" I pouted. "Because you can save it. My liver may thank you, but the rest of me doesn't."

"No lecture. You wanted to talk, remember?"

"I did? Oh, yeah." He fired up the engine and reversed, swinging the truck wide and out of the lot. We were both silent as we drove through town. It wasn't until the township was fading lights in the rearview mirror that he spoke again.

"Tell me what's bothering you."

I sighed. Loudly. Took a swig of whiskey from the bottle and wiped my mouth with the back of my arm.

"Okay, let me guess. It's SIA related."

"How do you do that?" I complained, waving the bottle at him.

"Because I'm a trained SIA agent who is good at reading people. And like it or not, Rae, you're an open book."

"You're not," I grumbled. "You're a teenager's journal, complete with lock and secret hiding place."

He laughed and patted my knee. "With training, you'll be able to read me. Anyone actually. Spit it out; what's the problem?"

"I found something."

This got his attention. His head swiveled toward me quickly before he returned his attention back to the road.

"About the case?" he asked.

I shrugged. "No. It's about my grandpa. And my dad."

"Oh?"

"You know, don't you?" I accused, hitting him in the shoulder.

"Ow. Cut it out. No, I don't know anything about your grandfather or your dad—except for what I've read in your file."

"Oh."

"What was it that you found?"

"It's better if I show you." Leaning my head

back, I closed my eyes, letting the rumble of the engine and sway of the truck lull me. I still wasn't sleeping well. Nightmares from my past haunted me, and I'd wake up shaking and crying for Grandpa. Only he wasn't here anymore—he was long gone—just the memory that shimmered out of my grasp as I reached for it.

When I'd eventually fall asleep again, Grandpa's memories were replaced by the horrors of the Institute and my time there. The pain. The abuse. The mind-numbing drugs. For years I'd carried the scars, physical as well as mental. Now the physical ones were gone, burned away by fire, but the mental ones would be with me forever. I guess it was true what they all said: I was one crazy psycho.

"Come on, sleepyhead, we're home." My door opened, and I almost tumbled out. Well, I would have if it weren't for my seatbelt holding me in place. It took a few embarrassingly long seconds for me to realize that the belt was the reason I couldn't get out. Jordan stood back, arms crossed, and watched.

"It feels weird calling you Jordan." Finally freeing myself, I slid out and slammed the door shut.

"I shudder to think what is going on in that brain of yours," was his response. At the front door, he studied my keys before inserting the correct one into the lock and opening the door.

He ushered me inside and then made his way to the kitchen, making himself at home.

"Coffee?" he asked.

"Are you kidding me? No. No, I do not want coffee. Why would I want coffee when I have this?" I waved the whiskey bottle at him. He sighed and got busy with the coffeemaker. I'd forgotten he knew this house, knew Grandma. He'd clearly made coffee in this kitchen many times before.

"You drink to forget, don't you?" he said, back to me. I sighed and sat on a kitchen stool, spinning the whiskey bottle around and around in front of me. I drank to forget, but I drank because I liked it. I liked the burn, and I liked the numbness, the dizziness. It took me out of myself—that's what I liked. But I could see where this was going. He wanted to save me. Only I couldn't be saved. I was damaged goods, and the sooner he realized that, the better.

"Don't tell me." I sneered. "You can help? There are better ways? Have I tried meditation? Yoga? Hypnosis?"

He glanced at me over his shoulder, surprise on his face. "Ouch."

I snorted. "Don't tell me that isn't where that

was going. I may be psycho, but I'm not stupid." He had the grace to look sheepish, and I spun the lid off the whiskey bottle and took another slug. Give up drinking? Never.

"What are all the boxes out front?" he asked, changing the subject. Smart man.

"Dad wanted me to pack up Grandpa's den. Which reminds me—I've changed my mind. He's not getting them. If he wants them, he can damn well come and pack them up himself." Sliding off the stool, I stomped to the front door and slammed it open, dragging the boxes back inside.

"O...kay." Jordan stood watching from the hallway, freshly made coffee in hand.

"There's something in these books he wants. I didn't realize it at first, but then I found the file, and then it all made perfect sense. I hadn't been looking, checking. I just chucked everything in and sealed the box, but now that I know...I have to check."

"Check for what? What file?"

"I'm pretty sure you know." There was an accusatory tone in my voice that I couldn't hide. He had been friends with Grandma. She'd told him all about our fire demon history. She had to have known Grandpa had been SIA. She would have told Jordan that. For sure.

"I swear I don't. I've already told you once, and I'm not going to beg you to believe me. I don't do begging."

"Shame." Lewd images danced through my head at the thought of Jordan begging.

"Now what are you thinking about?" Oh, he knew; the way his eyes had darkened told me he was thinking exactly the same thing, only he wanted me to say it. I wasn't going to make it that easy for him.

"What color to paint the den. Now that I'm clearing it out, I may as well renovate."

My sudden change in subject took him by surprise. His eyes widened, then narrowed, and he hid a grin behind his coffee cup.

"Will you keep the furniture?" he asked, following me into the den, where I pushed the box and left it in the middle of the floor.

"I don't think so. It's so dark and heavy and worn out. I like lighter stuff. White maybe? I may even turn this into my bedroom. I don't know yet."

"No more plans of leaving, then?"

"I tried and failed and have a great big bloody fine to show for my troubles. It seemed important to Grandma that I stay—I'll give it my best shot." It was true. I'd reconciled to the idea that I was here to stay, for a year at least. I'd texted a friend in

Fairbanks and asked them to pack up my apartment, sell the shitty furniture, box up what was left, and send it to me. Keep the winter gear. It wouldn't be needed in Maxxan.

I'd also noticed my demon wasn't as out of control as I remembered. I'd had a couple of flare-ups, but nothing like my youth. Combined with the training I'd done with Jordan, I finally felt like I had a grip on things. Even if it was a tenuous grip, it was better than flailing around with no hold on reality.

"Ready to tell me about your grandfather?" Jordan settled onto the worn Chesterfield, arm along the back, the other balancing the coffee mug on his knee.

"Wait here." Putting the whiskey bottle on the floor, I rushed upstairs, retrieved the file from under my mattress, and returned, standing in front of Jordan with it clutched to my chest.

"I found this. Hidden. Under the floorboards." I was breathless, puffing. He leaned forward but didn't try to take the file.

"Does that say…"

"SIA," I supplied.

"Ah." He nodded. "Hence your questions about the SIA. So, your grandfather was an agent?"

"I think so. Here." I handed the file to him, then

turned my attention to the box I'd dragged back inside. Ripping it open, I tipped it upside down, and all the books tumbled to the floor. Sitting cross-legged, I picked each one up and flicked through it, turned it upside down, and shook it, searching for anything that might be hidden inside. When nothing fell out, I placed it back in the box. I continued searching the books while Jordan read the file. It wasn't a particularly thick file, so it didn't take long before he'd closed it and placed it on the sofa next to him. He looked at me.

"I can see why you'd be rattled," he said.

"He suspected my dad."

Jordan nodded. "Yup."

"Of something, but he never said what? I guess he thought he had all the time in the world to conduct his investigation."

"Probably."

"Is that the best you've got? One-word answers? This is big. Huge! My grandfather was investigating my father! And then he was killed."

Silence, thick and heavy, descended over us. I was rapidly losing my buzz and eyed the whiskey bottle. Top up or sober up? Those were my options. The mood in the room was somber, and as tempting as that whiskey bottle was, I resisted. I felt like there should have been fireworks and confetti falling from the sky at this point, like I'd had a significant epiphany or something. Still, nothing was forthcoming, and I looked at Jordan in disappointment. Of course, he misunderstood because, apparently, he couldn't read my mind.

"I honestly didn't know about any of this, Rae," he said. "I don't think your grandmother did either, or she would have mentioned it to me. We talked a lot. She told me everything she knew of your family's history, what it meant to be a fire demon, but she was human. She only knew so much. And one of the SIA's number one priorities is to keep the public from finding out about paranormals." He looked around. "And you say your dad wants the contents of the den?"

"Yeah. Mom called. He didn't have the balls to call me himself. I was instructed to pack everything up, bar the furniture, and leave it in boxes out the front."

"He's searching for something. I wonder if he knew his dad was SIA?"

I pinched the top of my nose, thinking. Hard. "Why now? Grandpa has been dead for over twenty years. Plenty of time to search this place. Why wait? It doesn't make any sense."

"No, it doesn't. Okay." Leaning forward, elbows on knees, now-empty coffee cup cradled between his palms, he thought out loud. "We know your grandfather thought your father was involved in something dodgy. Illegal—from a paranormal perspective. Then your grandfather is killed. But it isn't until now, when your grandmother has died, that your dad has shown an interest in the contents of this room."

"So, it's doubtful Dad knew Grandpa was SIA. Otherwise, he'd have turned this room upside down as soon as he'd died."

"I agree. So why now? Coincidence? Or is he totally innocent, and it is what it looks like on the surface—a son wanting to retain his family's history?"

"The contents of the house go equally between Dad and my uncles. They had to sort it out themselves. My aunts have already started the process. You've seen that. I'm not sure my uncles even know that Dad is cleaning out the den."

"Let's see if we can find what he was looking for, then." Easing to the floor in front of me, Jordan mimicked my cross-legged position, and together we began searching through the books.

"We could be here all night," I warned.

"If that's what it takes," he replied. I smiled. I liked this man. My smile died—the thought alone was terrifying. Liking someone was the first step on the road to love, and with love came pain. It was a road I did not want to travel.

THIRTEEN

I panicked. It was what I do best. Instead of telling him that it was okay and he could leave, I dropped the book in my hands, cupped his face in my palms, and kissed him. I saw the flash of surprise on his face a second before I locked my lips on his. Then my eyes fluttered closed as the familiar heat that was him surrounded me and dragged me under.

He was ambrosia to me. I couldn't explain it, even if I tried. I'd kissed plenty of boys. Men. But none of them had the effect that Jordan had. The sizzling of my blood, the pounding of my heart, the tingling that robbed my brain of all reasoning. All from one kiss.

His hand reached out, wrapped around my neck.

The other slid around my back and pulled me closer to him. We devoured each other, all mouths and tongues, hands exploring. I eased away slightly, my fingers gripping the hem of his T-shirt and tugging it up. He obliged, pulling away long enough to pull it over his head and toss it aside before his mouth was back on mine. His fingers curled in my hair and pulled, and I groaned my delight while my fingers explored the expanse of his chest, loving the way his abs were so tight beneath my fingertips.

We were on the floor when he paused and looked down at me, those dark eyes of his mesmerizing.

"Why are you stopping?" I breathed. "Don't stop."

"Rae." The way he said my name, his voice full of regret. I froze, tensing beneath him. He felt it and eased up, sitting on his haunches.

"Sorry. Could have sworn you wanted me." I hid my hurt beneath sarcasm.

"I do. I want you like you wouldn't believe," he muttered through gritted teeth.

"Then why stop?" I didn't understand. He wanted me. I was ready and willing. More than willing.

"I don't want to take advantage of you...and..."

"What?" I scrambled away from him.

"And I don't want a one-night stand with you."

This was about morals? What century was he living in? "Are you serious?"

"I don't want to be another notch on your bedpost, Rae—and don't bullshit me by telling me you don't have a very impressive list of past lovers."

"I wouldn't call them impressive." Most of them had been average at best. "You don't want to sleep with me because I've had too many lovers?" Judgey bastard.

"I don't care about your past." He was shaking his head and climbed to his feet, searching for his T-shirt. "I'm more interested in your future. You're the hit it and quit it type."

"Didn't know that was a crime." I stood, at a loss to know what to do with my aching body.

"You're not hearing me."

"Because you're talking shit!" My voice rose with my frustration.

Crossing the room in long strides, he backed me up against an empty bookcase, and my heart leaped with desire. This was more like it.

"I want you, Rae. More than you know. I want all of you. Not just your body, and not just for one night. I want you—body, mind, and soul. I want you to be *mine*."

"You want a...*relationship*?" I was aghast.

He inclined his head. "I do. I want forever. Because you and I, Rae? We're fated."

"Get out," I whispered, trembling. How dare he? How dare he ask that of me? He said he knew me, but he didn't know me at all.

"Rae—" He touched my cheek, but I pushed him away, my anger flaring.

"Get out!" My scream bounced from the walls, so loud I winced. Without a word, he swiveled and left, the front door closing with a quiet click. I stood chest-heaving, mind whirling. I waited to hear the sound of his truck starting until I remembered he didn't have a truck. He'd driven mine. So, the bastard had to walk. Good.

Finding my top, I pulled it over my head, uncaring that it was inside out. Sinking back down on the floor, I grabbed the whiskey bottle and guzzled until I had to stop to draw a breath. Better. Numbing. I needed the numbness, so I didn't have to think. It was true. I didn't do relationships. Not anymore. Because I fucked them up. I'd do something stupid, and I'd get dumped, and it hurt. It hurt that someone you liked, possibly could fall in love with, would turn with hate in their eyes and scream at you that you were indeed a crazy fucked up psycho. And yet I'd tried countless times, and I couldn't blame the guy because it was all me. I'd flirt, I'd cheat, I'd sabotaged every relationship I ever had. I was horrible. I was a horrible person.

Guzzling more from the whiskey bottle, I batted at the stray tear winding its way down my cheek. Picking up the next book in the pile, I resumed the search. I'd focus on finding out what Dad's secret was and nothing else. Not how hot Jordan Buchanan is, or his crazy belief that we're fated. Fated mates, my ass. There was no such thing.

A GOD-AWFUL BANGING noise jerked me awake, and I sat up, peeling a book from my cheek. With aching joints, I pushed to my feet. I'd fallen asleep on a pile of books in the den. The banging at the front door continued, and I yelled, "Okay, okay." Wincing at the throbbing in my head.

Flinging open the door, I frowned at Paige, who stood looking perky and fresh in a floral dress, her hair pulled up in a high ponytail and swinging down her back with each movement of her head. Her cuteness made me want to hurl.

"Big night?" she asked, pushing past me with a cardboard tray carrying two takeaway coffees and a brown paper bag.

"Who told you?"

"Jesus. Look at this place." Paige stood and looked around the stripped kitchen and dining room.

I gestured at the walls. "Weird, huh?"

"So weird. Cam said you'd started painting?"

"Did the living room. Wanna see?" I waved down the hallway. Paige set the tray on the kitchen bench, and I snatched up a coffee while she stuck her head in the living room door. "Looks good," she called out.

"Thanks." Opening the bag, I peered inside. The smell hitting my nostrils had my stomach growling.

"Bacon and egg sandwich. He called you, didn't he?" It wasn't a question. Jordan had definitely called Paige.

"He was...concerned." She grinned unapologetically. "He cares about you, Rae."

"Yeah, well, he shouldn't. We all know it won't end well."

"Oh, ye of little faith." She scoffed, removing the

second sandwich from the bag and taking a bite. "What are you so afraid of?"

"That I'll fuck it up. I always do. And then you'll all be angry with me for driving him away. Don't think I don't know that y'all are friends with him. Hell, even Grandma was friends with him."

"He's a good guy."

"He probably is. But I'm not good for him."

Paige reached out and grabbed my hand. "Rae, you may not have noticed this because you're... well...you're you—but...you've changed. You're making an effort. The old you would have been on the first bus out of Maxxan without a backward glance, not giving a shit about Grandma's wishes, but look at you, still here, pimping up the house."

I cringed. "Paige, I tried to leave. I had a ticket on the eight-a.m. bus. If it hadn't been for the sheriff booking me, I'd have been long gone. You're seeing what you want to see: a reformed Shelton. I don't think I can ever be reformed."

Her eyes welled, and I felt like I'd kicked a puppy. "You don't see it, do you?" she muttered, voice tight. "How much they damaged you? Grandma was right. You should never have been locked away. They tried to fix something that wasn't broken, and in the end, they broke you."

I was shaking my head. "Paige, honey, I was a psycho. I still am."

"No. You're not. Honest to God, you're not. They made you this way. The institute. They drilled it into you that you're damaged, broken, that everything that happened was your fault."

"It was."

"I can prove it," she said smugly, folding her arms across her chest.

"How?"

"Grandma found Grandpa's book of demons."

"Book of what now?"

"It's like...a book of instructions for being a fire demon. A bible almost, but not for scripture. It has our history. Our story. But also, our biology, and what happens if our demon activates early."

"What are you even talking about?" Maybe Paige was the crazy one?

"Grandma hinted at it in her letter to you. When a fire demon reaches eighteen years of age, they come into their powers. A child cannot control them, so it's genetically wired to kick in at eighteen. But...your powers came in when you were five. You experienced a traumatic event; your life was in danger, and your demon stepped in to save you. A basic response. Only no one knew. Grandpa would have known straight away, but he was dead. Your dad and uncles didn't know better. They were eighteen when their powers materialized. It had been easy for them. And so here you were, a little girl with powers she couldn't possibly control, with no one to help her, who was constantly punished."

I contemplated what Paige said. It sounded plausible, but I needed to see it for myself.

"Where is this book?"

"In Grandma's room."

Damn. My mom and aunties had already cleared out her room. Now they must have it, but Paige was already grinning and shaking her head.

"She hid it. She didn't want any of the olds to have it. She was angry at them for what happened to you, and she'd argued with them dozens of times over it, but our fathers shot her down each and every time because she's a human, and what would she know?"

Holy. Fucking. Shit.

"Shall we go look?" she asked. I was out the door before she'd finished talking. With Paige hot on my heels, we scrambled up the stairs, stopping in front of Grandma's bedroom door. I still couldn't bring myself to open it. Paige had no qualms, though.

Pushing me aside, she thrust the door open and strode inside.

"They really did clear everything out, didn't they?" She shook her head, hands-on-hips, as she surveyed the room. Grandma's scent was gone, and I was kinda sad. Wardrobe doors stood open, dresser drawers too. Everything was gone bar the furniture and mattress. They'd even taken the bedding.

"So, where did she hide it?" I asked.

"Here." Crossing to the big heavy tallboy, she pulled the bottom drawer all the way out, placed it on the floor, and then reached her hand in. I heard a click, and then a section of the side of the tallboy popped out. A secret compartment! Paige pulled out a worn leather-bound book and grinned at me triumphantly.

"See? I knew they wouldn't find it. Grandma specifically said in her will that they couldn't take the furniture, only the contents. She wanted us to find it. She wanted you to have it."

"Why not just give it to that lawyer, the executor, and have him give it to me?"

"Why indeed? Maybe she didn't trust him? Maybe it was too risky? I don't know, but I do know we have it. Here." She held it out to me, and I took it from her.

"How do you know about it?"

"Grandma told me. When she got sick. She said her time was up, and we kids needed to know our true history, our heritage and that she was worried our parents were more interested in suppressing our fire demon side rather than embracing it. She swore me to secrecy."

"No one else knows?"

"No one."

"Grandma, you were the original renegade." I smiled, hugging the book to my chest. She'd taken a chance, all those years ago, a human girl loving a fire demon, starting a life with him, shunned by family and friends. My mind boggled at what a strong person she'd been, how difficult life must have been for them, moving to a town where everyone was a stranger and Grandpa having to hide what he really was. I wondered if it had been difficult for him or easier back then, before cell phones, cameras, and social media.

Sitting on the mattress together, we thumbed through the pages. The handwriting changed several times, and I realized this had been put together by Grandpa's family—it really was the story of our heritage, our powers. I stopped on a page with a sketch of a young man with fire in his hands that stretched out several meters in front of him. Around the fire were arrows, indicating the fire was traveling back toward the man.

"What's this?" I whispered, running my finger along the lines of text.

"We can control our fire?" Paige whispered in response.

"It looks that way. Look, he's using it like a whip!" *Mind blown.* I'd only just learned to summon and suppress my fire. I could command it to a certain extent, push it away, and call it back, but the image on the page showed a man wielding it like a lasso. Turning the page, I frowned—more surprises.

"Blue fire?" Paige questioned. I was as puzzled as she, but there it was, all laid out before us. Turned out we could turn our fire cold...icy, in fact. So rather than burn, we could freeze. On and on, the surprises went on about what was truly possible as a fire demon. We could command our fire not to burn, not to harm. We could consume ourselves in flame and heal—I'd already discovered that one by accident.

"We have to tell the others." Paige flopped back on the bed, staring up at the ceiling. I joined her.

"Do you think we can do all those things?" I patted the book. "We're not full-blooded fire demons. Maybe our powers are diluted."

"Only one way to find out." Her grin was cheeky, and her eyes twinkled.

"No. Not today. Let's get the others, and we can practice and learn together."

"Jordan can help." She was nodding.

"You call him Jordan?" I sat up, clutching the book to my chest. On the front were the words Fire Slinger.

"Well, yeah, it's his name. Why, what do you call him?" she asked, then grabbed my arm. "No, wait, don't tell me. You call him asshole? Or douchebag?"

I cringed. Those were some of my more popular names for people.

"Not to his face." Handing the book to Paige, I told her to wait, then retrieved the file from downstairs.

"What's this?" she asked, looking from the file to me and back again.

"Something I found of Grandpa's. He went to a lot of trouble to keep it hidden, so I think we should do the same. Put it with the book." I handed it to her and watched as she slid them both back into the secret compartment, closed it, and slid the drawer back in.

"Something is going on in Maxxan," I said, not

sure how much Paige knew, "and...I'm not sure who we can trust."

"You trust me, though, right?"

"Of course I do, silly." I gave her a squeeze. "But I'm not sure how much our parents know." I didn't want to tell her about my dad. Not until I knew for sure. Maybe it was all nothing. Whatever Grandpa had thought he was involved in could have all blown over by now.

"I agree. Grandma never told them about this book—clearly, she didn't want them to know; otherwise, she would have given it to them years ago."

"Right. So we tell Cam and Tyler. What about Cody?" Cody was Paige's brother and the only other Shelton currently residing in Maxxan. Her sister Katie and our cousins Vanessa and Travis all lived in Redmeadows. They'd returned briefly for Grandma's funeral and had promptly left again.

"Yes, Cody needs to know. Just the five of us, then. And Jordan. That makes six."

"Let's invite them for dinner under the ruse of helping with the renovations you're doing. We can say you need some help moving furniture around," Paige suggested.

"Actually, that's true. I do need some help

moving furniture around. I'm going to give some of it away. I guess you guys get first dibs."

"Make sure you search everything for secret compartments," Paige warned. "I have a feeling this house has a few more secrets concealed within its walls."

"Who knew, eh?" I stretched, then groaned. "Man, I've got to take a shower."

"You do that. Then we'll head to town to get supplies for tonight."

"Deal. Will you text the boys?"

"Already done." Her fingers were flying across the screen of her phone as she spoke.

"I won't be long. If you want something to do while you're waiting, I was searching the books in the den." I briefly filled her in on finding Grandpa's hiding spot without divulging that I thought there was a high possibility my dad was a bad guy—just that I wanted to check the books before packing them up. She bought it, thankfully.

In the bathroom, I eyed myself critically in the mirror. The sleep deprivation was showing in the purple shadows under my eyes. I still hadn't gotten used to my scars being gone. I ran my fingers over the smooth expanse of my shoulder where a jagged scar had been before—the result of a stabbing at the institute by another inmate. It never had healed properly, and I'd had constant pain in that shoulder, but now? All healed, no pain. It was as if it had never happened.

Stepping beneath the spray, I quickly washed, noticing how my skin was no longer lily-white but back to my semi-tanned self. All over. Apparently, this was my natural skin tone now that I'd bathed in my own flames. And the heat of Maxxan no longer bothered me. I hadn't really noticed before, but I'd stopped sweating profusely and flushing in the heat. I'd adjusted, and I was actually okay with it. Before returning, I'd been terrified of what would happen being back home, but now? Now that we had Grandpa's Fire Slinger book with everything we could ever need to know about fire demons, I actually felt excited.

"All set?" I asked, watching Paige from the doorway of the den. She sat where I'd sat the night before, cross-legged on the floor. Glancing up, she smiled at me and jumped to her feet.

"Sure. The boys are in, by the way." She wriggled her phone at me.

"Great." Leading the way outside, I stopped in my tracks when I spotted a neatly folded pile of clothes with a pair of boots on top.

"Are they...?" Paige looked from the pile of clothes to me. "Jordan's?"

"They must be," I admitted. "He gave me a lift home last night. He must have shifted to get home himself." I was sorry I'd missed it.

"He didn't stay over then?"

"I thought he called you?"

"He did. Told me you could probably use some TLC today and that it would be better received coming from me than him. Come on, spit it out. What happened?"

I debated whether to tell her or not. I wasn't usually one to discuss my private life, but Paige was family, and I'd missed having someone I could confide in. "Things were getting hot and heavy, and then he stopped. Apparently, he didn't want to take advantage of me."

"Because you were drunk?"

"That and the fact that I'm a hit it and quit it type of gal—his words—and that didn't suit him."

"Well...that's good, isn't it? He wants something more...permanent?"

"He says we're fated mates," I blurted.

"Oh my God!" Paige squealed, making me jump. "Rae, that is wonderful! Congratulations!"

"No!" I shouted, and she looked at me in shock.

"No way. This isn't happening, Paige. Not with him. Not with anyone. I'm a disaster. I'll ruin it. No. It's better to walk away now rather than later when I'm so invested it'll kill me to lose him."

"Oh, Rae." Paige wrapped her arms around me and squeezed, and I had to swallow back the lump of emotion stuck in my throat. "You can't run from fated mates." Her voice was soft, her hand soothing as it rubbed up and down my spine. "You'll be fine. If the fates have chosen him for you, then it's a good match. Trust in that."

I opened my mouth to argue when I spotted it, just outside the front gate. The hellhound. It saw me and sat, mouth open, tongue lolling out.

"Um, Paige?" I breathed the words in her ear, grabbing hold and squeezing tight when she would have pulled back to look at me. "Don't make any sudden moves, and for the love of God, just do as I say and don't argue."

"What's happening?" she whispered, my tone telling her I wasn't messing around.

"Hellhound."

"Where?" She turned her head to look.

"You can't see it?"

"No."

Strange. But I didn't have time to dwell on it. I

had to get Paige out of here. We could go back inside, but I had no idea if hellhounds could bust open doors. Too risky. If it was here, it was after me. Paige would be collateral damage.

"What's the plan?" she whispered, voice calm.

"Get you safely in your car and out of here."

"What about you?"

"It's me it wants. If I go with you, it'll only follow. Call Jordan once you're out of sight."

"Okay."

I cupped her chin and eyeballed her. "I mean it, Paige. No messing around. Get in your car, get out of here. *Then* call for help. Understood?"

She nodded, and I had to believe she'd do the right thing. I was worried if she sat in her car for one second too long, the hellhound would be upon her.

"How are we doing this?" she asked. I was surprised—and proud—of how calm she was.

"I'm going to lead it away, behind the house. Once I'm out of sight, count to twenty, then go. As quietly as you can."

"Got it."

Leaving Paige on the steps, I walked toward the hellhound who sat passively watching me. Halfway down the path, I veered to the right, following the overgrown track that led to the rear of the house. I watched out of the corner of my eye, and sure enough, the hellhound stood and began to follow, keeping to the perimeter of the fence. Not that the fence was of any use whatsoever; it held no functional purpose other than to mark the start and end of Grandma's front garden, for the fence didn't wrap around the house. Once the hellhound reached the end, there would be nothing between me and it but a few garden plants and weeds.

I picked up my pace, turning down the side of the house, hurrying even further to reach the back garden. I could hear the hellhound breathing as it followed, keeping its distance. I took that as a good sign. If it wanted to kill me, it would have attacked as soon as I'd left the house. I assumed. I didn't know much about hellhounds other than they were a really big dog from hell. Besides me being the only one who could apparently see it, that was the extent of my knowledge. I didn't know *why* I was the only one or what it could mean. Maybe I was about to find out.

Standing in the back garden in the scorched patch of grass, I waited. I heard Paige's car start up and then drive away, relieved when the hellhound paid zero attention, instead approaching me and stopping mere feet away. His coloring was striking, a mottled brown and black, with green eyes. I'd thought they'd be red.

"So," I said out loud, not knowing what to do next. Did these things talk? I waited, but got no response.

"What do you want?" I tried again. The hound tilted his head to one side, not taking his eyes off me.

"You look like a Rottweiler," I told it, "only like three times bigger." When its tail thumped the ground, I just about peed myself. Then I realized it was wagging its tail!

"Are you...happy?" I asked. This time, the head tilted the other way, and I chuckled. He was cute as fuck. If not a shit ton of scary.

"Umm. Nice doggie?" I tried again, but was pretty sure the creature couldn't speak. My theory was confirmed when a deep rumbling *woof* came my way, making the ground vibrate beneath my feet. A full-blown bark would have probably knocked me over. Sucking in a breath and blowing it out, I took a tentative step toward the hound. It passively watched me, its tail still thumping on the ground behind it. I got as close as I dared and stretched out my hand, screwing my eyes closed. This was make or break. It was either going to bite my hand off or not. I wondered if I had the ability as a fire demon to re-grow limbs. I also didn't think it was a good idea to find out.

When a big wet snout nuzzled my hand, my eyes popped open, and my mouth dropped open in surprise. The big scary beast was head-butting my hand and wanting to be petted.

"Hey, big boy," I murmured, stroking my hand across the top of his head. His tail thumped even harder, and when I scratched behind his ear, he dropped to the ground, rolled over, and presented his belly for belly rubs.

"That was unexpected." I laughed, then leaned over and obliged. Before long, I was on the ground, a massive dog head in my lap as I stroked his fur and told him what a beautiful boy he was.

"I'm not sure that's wise," Jordan said from the back door. I glanced over my shoulder. "You can see him?"

"I can."

"I wonder why that is?" The hound lifted his head and sniffed the air, his eyes zeroing in on Jordan. He growled, a fierce, terrifying sound.

"Easy, boy, easy." To my surprise, he complied. The growling stopped, and he flopped his head back into my lap.

"I think he's yours now." Jordan stepped down from the porch and slowly made his way towards us. The hound paid zero attention to him, nudging my hand again for more pats.

"I've never had a pet before," I admitted, eyeing the massive creature.

"Trust you to start with a hellhound."

"I don't know anything about them. Do you?"

"No, but I'll find out." Pulling out his phone, he walked away, the phone to his ear, voice low.

"So. We're going to have to come up with a name for you," I told the hound, laughing when he softly woofed in apparent agreement. "What do I feed you? You're incorporeal, so not real food, I'm assuming."

"You don't need to feed him anything." Jordan was back. Crouching in front of me, he gave the hound a stroke on the head. The hound cracked open one eye to look at him, gave his hand a sniff, then closed his eyes again, and was more than happy for Jordan to lavish him with attention.

"He's just a big dog. A big softie dog." I laughed. "How did he get here?"

Jordan cocked his head to one side. "I don't know how the vampires managed to summon one, but clearly, he's decided that he belongs to you and not them."

"What did you find out? How do I look after him?" I was surprisingly and instantly attached to my giant dog.

"You don't need to do anything. When he's hungry, he'll feed off the souls of the dead or dying."

"I can't have him killing people," I protested.

"He won't. They don't kill. They're hunters, trackers. He sniffs out the prey but doesn't do the killing. When he needs to, he'll feed on the soul of the prey, but that isn't every kill. Maybe only once a year."

"Hmmm. I hope he likes rogue vampire souls," I grumbled, not happy that souls were his food source but relieved that he wasn't a killer.

FOURTEEN

I thought it would be awkward seeing Jordan again, but Bear's arrival eased any tensions—at least as far as I was concerned. I'd decided on calling my new hellhound Bear, given he closely resembled one. Only bigger. It was either Bear or Dog.

"When you're done rolling around on the dirt with the hound, we've got work to do." His voice didn't hold any particular inflection, yet there was something in it that had me tilting my head and studying him. If he wanted to talk about the fated mate thing, I'd sic Bear on him.

"Yes, boss." I climbed to my feet and dusted off my jeans. Bear sat next to me. Even sitting, he was as tall as me. "What's the plan for today?"

"One of the vampires we captured has started talking. He says the big boss is heading to Maxxan—is possibly already here."

"And do we know who this big boss is?"

"Apparently, he goes by the name Gunslinger."

"Wait!" I exclaimed. "Isn't that the name—?"

"—that was in your grandfather's file? Yes, I do believe it was."

"So, this Gunslinger dude is returning? Do we know why?"

"To *sort shit out* is the response we received," Jordan replied.

"And you want to try to find him? But how? They blend in; they look like us; they walk in the daylight. And they're smart enough not to attack me walking down the street."

"I know where you're going with this, and it's not going to happen." He eyed me up and down, his gaze hot, distracting. "We will not be using you as bait. But I do think Paige is right. This house has more secrets to reveal. I say we start searching. How's the den going? Got through all those books yet?"

"Fell asleep in the middle of it last night." Leading the way inside, I'd kind of forgotten about

Bear until he walked right through the door behind us. It was disconcerting, to say the least.

"So, hellhounds don't have the same limitations as vampires. Good to know." I nodded, gave Bear a pat, then headed into the den.

Jordan stopped in the doorway and eyed the books, then me. I swear to God, his cheeks flushed. Was he thinking about last night? Because now I was, damn it.

"Rae." It was a sigh, a groan, a plea, all in one. How was a girl meant to cope with this amount of hotness standing right in front of her?

"Maybe you should check out the furniture in the rest of the house?" I suggested. "See if you can find any more secret compartments." My way of dealing? Send the temptation away. Far, far away. I didn't take rejection well. His leaving me extremely unsatisfied last night, despite his wild claims, did not put him in my "favorite person" category. But we had to work together, and this was the best I could offer him.

"If that's what you want."

"It's what I want." Settling myself in the den, I got busy sorting through the books. Bear did his best to lie on the sofa, but the hellhound just wouldn't fit.

He finally gave up and sprawled on the floor in front of it. I leaned back against him, and there we stayed, flicking through book after book, finding nothing but dust and the odd scrap of paper that I assumed had been used as a bookmark once upon a time.

It wasn't until Bear lifted his head and let out a long, low, rumbling growl that I stopped.

"What is it, boy?" He barked. Just the once, but that was enough to rattle the windows.

"Okay, okay, shhh. Let's go see." Standing, I walked to the front door, Bear squeezing in next to me so that he just about shoved me into the wall. "Come on, dog, you're the incorporeal one, not me. You walk through the wall and give us both some room."

Just as I opened the front door, I heard it. A car pulling up. A flurry of dust appeared, followed by the slamming of a door and footsteps running toward the house.

"Tyler? What's wrong?"

"Holy fuck!" Tyler skidded to a halt, back-peddling with his arms waving. "What the hell is that?"

"Oh, you can see him? Okay, well, this is my dog, Bear."

"*That* is not a dog."

"Technically, a hellhound."

"And you have a hellhound because…?"

"He adopted me," I explained. "Back to you. What's the rush?"

"Shit. Yeah. It's Mom. She's missing!"

"What? You took the time to drive here? Why didn't you call me?" My voice rose, and so did Bear's hackles. I patted him absently, not wanting him to rip my little brother to shreds.

"I tried. Straight to voice mail. Is your phone dead?"

Digging in my back pocket, I pulled out my phone, swiped the screen, and sure enough. Absolutely nothing. Damn it, I cast my mind back, trying to remember the last time I'd charged it.

"It doesn't matter," Tyler cried. "Mom does."

"What's going on?" Jordan joined us, and Tyler repeated what he'd told me.

"You think she's been taken?"

Tyler nodded. "Her car door was open, engine running, still in the driveway. Her purse was on the ground a few feet away. There was blood."

"Blood? A lot?" I piped up. Tyler was already shaking his head. "No. Just a few drops."

"We've got this," I said to Jordan, jogging toward the gate, Bear hot on my heels.

"Rae, hold up. You can't go running off half-cocked. We don't know where they've taken her!" Jordan ran after me, with Tyler trailing behind.

"We've got a secret weapon." I cocked my head at Bear. "I'm taking him out to Mom's to pick up her scent. He can lead us straight to them. And help bring them down."

"Okay, well—"

Before he could finish, I was in my truck. Bear jumped into the tray, and we were off, gunning it down the driveway in a cloud of dust. I don't know why the vampires kept messing with my family, but it had to stop. Now that I had their own weapon to use against them, I had every confidence getting my mom back would be relatively easy.

I flew down the back roads to Mom and Dad's. Every time I glanced in the rearview mirror, all I could see was Bear's massive chest. I assumed his head was above the cab, enjoying the wind in his face like most dogs liked to do. A glance in the side mirrors showed Jordan's nark mobile not too far behind. I assumed Tyler was with him.

Pulling up out front of Mom's house, I'd barely stopped moving when Bear jumped down and began sniffing the ground. In a matter of seconds, he'd found the drops of blood Tyler had mentioned and stood, nose an inch from the ground, breathing in the scent. Then he lifted his big head and barked twice.

"Yes, good boy, yes. Go find her. I'll follow." Bear was off, and I was back in my truck and following him before Jordan had a chance to catch up. I hoped I was doing the right thing using Bear to track Mom. It worried me that maybe he'd thought I meant she was dinner, and he had to go find her so he could devour her soul. That just spurred me to drive faster and not lose the giant hound as he bounded across fields at an incredible pace.

They hadn't taken a direct route. We'd backtracked more than once, driven in a complete circle twice, and pretty much wound our way through the entire county of Maxxan before Bear came to a halt, sitting on his haunches at the end of a long dirt track in what appeared to be the middle of nowhere. Pulling my truck off the side of the road, I killed the engine and climbed out, closing the door as quietly as I could behind me.

"You think she's here, boy?" I patted Bear and squinted down the track. I could just make out a roof on the horizon. We were out in farmland, fields with swaying crops of cotton and hay surrounding us. Maybe they were holding her in an old farmhouse or barn. They'd either been invited in, or whoever owned the property was no longer in the land of the living; otherwise, the vampires wouldn't be able to enter.

Jordan pulled up behind me. "Have you come up with a plan yet?" he asked, tongue in cheek.

"Haha. Plans are your department."

"I thought so too until you went running off tracking your mom without any idea of what you'd do next." His arms were crossed over his chest, and he didn't look pleased.

"I've got Bear," I said defensively. "Plus, these assholes have got to learn to stop taking my fucking family."

"And how do you plan on teaching them a lesson?"

"Okay, listen up." I whirled on him, worry for my mom pushing my anger and intolerance levels sky-high. "I do not need your attitude right now. I need your help. You keep saying you're SIA, well, SIA my mom's ass out of there."

"Whoa, burned." Tyler snickered, then shut up when Jordan shot him a look.

"Here's what we do." Jordan's face was a mask. I couldn't tell if he was pissed at my outburst. I didn't have time to worry about it now. He was heading toward the back of his vehicle, and we both followed. Bear stayed put, keeping a keen eye on the building in the distance.

"Tyler." Jordan handed him a pyre gun. "Stick with me. You can shoot, right?"

"Yeah, I can shoot." Tyler puffed his chest out, pleased to be included in the action.

"Rae, I assume Bear will stick with you, give you an extra level of protection, but take this anyway." He handed me a pyre gun. "And for the love of God, keep your eyes open."

"I will." Geez. One time, one time you fire a gun with your eyes closed, and they never let you forget it.

"And don't forget—both of you—that you have fire demon skills. Use them. Rae, stay focused. You know you can do it. Burn them if you have to—it won't kill them, but it will incapacitate them long enough for us to either get your mother out or take them down."

"Mom's human." It felt like the right time to remind him of that. I could easily burn my mother to a crisp.

"I'll protect her. I won't let you burn her." I trusted the confidence in his voice.

"You and Bear go that way; head around the

back." He pointed, and I nodded. "Tyler and I will come in the front. You should have the advantage of surprise. And hopefully, they don't know Bear has changed sides yet. Assuming he has."

"Wait. What? You think Bear isn't legit?" I stopped Jordan before he could walk away. "You think they planted him?"

"No." Jordan shook his head and cupped my cheek, seeing the worry on my face. I was uncharacteristically attached to the hellhound. It would break my heart if it turned out it was all a ruse. "I don't believe that at all. I think he's here because he wants to be. Something about you attracted him, and now that he's attached himself, the rest of us can see him."

It made sense. No one had been able to see the hellhound before, only me. But as soon as we decided we were friends, that I would keep him as my own, Jordan could see him, and Tyler could see him. I could only guess that the rest of my family would be able to see him, too, because they were all connected to me. I wondered what I did to become so important.

"Let's go. Wait for my signal," Jordan said.

Shit! Had I been daydreaming? "What signal?" I

asked. He shook his head, grabbed my shoulders, and leaned down so his face was level with mine.

"I will create a distraction out front. Draw them out. As soon as I do, I want you to slip in the back and get your mom out," he said with exaggerated patience.

"You're assuming there's a back entrance?"

"I've cased all the abandoned farmhouses in Maxxan. Vampires are holed up in several of them. The farmhouse on this property was burned down. All that's left is the barn. I suspect that's where your mom is. It has doors at both ends."

"Gotcha." Before I could pull away, he planted a fast and hard kiss on my lips, then swiveled on his heel and headed down the driveway with Tyler by his side.

"Wow," I whispered, touching my lips. Even such a brief kiss sizzled. Shaking myself, I whistled to Bear, and the two of us headed through the hayfield toward the back of the barn. I worried that Jordan would be in place, and we were still traipsing through the field when Bear solved that problem by coming up behind me, shoving his nose between my knees, and tossing me over his head. Before I knew it, I was sitting on the hellhound's shoulders and riding him like a horse. *Un-fucking-believable.*

We arrived at the rear of the barn on silent feet —riding a hellhound had its advantages. Sliding off Bear's back, I tiptoed to the barn and peered inside. I spied Mom, tied to a beam in the middle of the barn. I could only see one vampire. I'd expected more, but then, this was most likely a trap, and as soon as we stepped inside, we'd be swarmed. Bear crossed to the other side of the door and sat, waiting for my signal.

"Two men, coming up the drive." A vampire rushed in, and both stood in the opposite doorway, watching Jordan and Tyler approach.

"Is one of 'em her husband?" the vampire that had been inside asked.

"Can't tell," the other replied.

Her husband? This was a trap for...Dad? I'd thought it was for me. After all, they'd taken Tyler to lure me out. But these two didn't seem too bright. They'd totally left the rear of the barn unprotected, even though its two big doors stood open, indicating it was an entrance. Idiots. Shaking my head, I leaned against the wall and waited. I could hear movement inside, but not enough to indicate a horde of vampires was waiting for us.

Then there was the sound of fighting, grunting, and bodies hitting the ground. I stuck my head in the doorway, and sure enough, Jordan was tussling with a vampire. The other vamp was standing in front of Mom, guarding her. So far, no one else had appeared. Nodding my head at Bear, I slipped inside. Bear walked beside me. I was almost to Mom when the vampire must have heard or sensed me and glanced around.

"You!" He snarled, leaping toward me. Tyler fired off his pyre gun but missed. Didn't matter. Bear raised a massive paw and swatted the vampire to the ground.

"What the fuck was that?" The vampire wriggled backward on the barn floor, looking around wildly. Good—he couldn't see Bear.

"That was me." I strolled forward, keeping one eye on the activity outside. The vampire continued to back up, and as I approached, I called forth my fire, tossing it between my palms. Then I thought about what I'd read in Grandpa's fire slinger book— wouldn't hurt to try, I guess? I pictured the flames turning into a lasso, and before my eyes, the flame turned into a long rope with a coil at the end. I tentatively gave it a whirl, and it swung, just like a rope would. Cool.

"Jesus." The vampire watched me, eyes wide.

"Wow!" I heard Tyler, and, without taking my

gaze from the vampire, I told him, "Get Mom. Take my truck. Get her home."

He ran past us and busied himself freeing Mom, who was sobbing. I wasn't sure if she was hurt or if they had bitten her, but she was alive, and I sent up a silent prayer of thanks.

"Now, you, what's your name?" I twirled the lasso over my head. The vamp had gotten over his shock and sneered at me.

"I ain't telling you nothin." He pushed himself to his feet and assumed a fighting stance. Excellent. I get to try out my new toy.

"You're right. I don't need your name. I don't care." With a flick of my wrist, the lasso sailed through the air and settled over his shoulders. I tightened it with a sharp tug.

The vampire screamed like a girl. High pitched and long. "It's burning!"

"Duh," I mocked. It was a lasso of fire. What was he expecting?

"Can't kill me with fire," he breathed, writhing at the end of my flame rope.

I tilted my head and examined him critically. "You know," I said conversationally, "I probably could if I just repositioned this around your neck—

and pulled. Your head would probably pop right off."

I heard Mom's startled gasp and frowned over my shoulder at Tyler. "Hurry up and get her out of here," I snapped. "She doesn't need to see this."

"Come on, Mom." Tyler slung an arm around her and began leading her out of the barn. They were as slow as molasses. With a sigh, I called to them, "Take Bear. It'll be faster."

"Take Bear?" Tyler asked, puzzled.

"Yeah. Climb on his back. Like a horse." I signaled to Bear, who was sitting behind me. "Bear. Lay." He did so, and Tyler reluctantly approached him.

"That's a really big dog," Mom whispered, her voice wobbling.

"It's okay. He won't hurt you. He's a gentle giant," I reassured her. Tyler climbed on Bear's back, then held down a hand for Mom, hauling her up behind him.

"Take her home, Bear," I instructed. "Slowly!" I yelled, knowing how he liked to travel at breakneck speeds. His slow was still faster than Tyler could run.

"What...what's going on?" the vampire stuttered. To him, it looked like Tyler, and my mom was suspended in midair and then floating away. I laughed. He must feel like he was on a bad acid trip. It was about to get worse.

"See, your first mistake," I said conversationally, tugging on the lasso and reeling him in closer, "was taking my mom. I assumed you did it to get to me, but seeing as you two knuckleheads appear to be here on your lonesome, I'm doubting that assumption. So spill. Why take my mom?"

"Boss wants Frank Shelton. There's a reward. Figured we'd draw him out by taking his missus."

Interesting. The vampires were after my dad and were using tactics such as this to get him. Which meant he wasn't working with them. Or maybe he had been, once, but wasn't anymore. The smell of burning flesh filled my nostrils, reminding me I had a vampire writhing at the end of my flaming lasso.

"Who's your boss?" I asked, tugging again. The vampire bellowed "bitch" which I took to be an insult and not the name of his boss.

Since my foray into my powers and what I could really do had gone so well, I decided to give it another shot. Instead of a flaming lasso, I thought of a freezing one. And as simple as that, with just a mere thought, the flames turned blue, the burning stopped, and the vampire started to freeze. With another flick, I moved the lasso from over his shoulders to around one wrist only. I didn't want to freeze his head; he wouldn't be able to give me the answers I wanted if that were the case.

Ignoring the vile names the vampire was calling me, I watched as his hand turned blue, then froze solid. Stepping forward, I seized one finger and snapped it off.

The sound the vampire made was...unsettling. I felt a little squeamish at what I'd just done, but I just had to remind myself what the vampires had done to my grandpa to push through it. Retribution would be mine.

"Who. Is. Your. Boss?" I seized another finger and snapped it off, tossing it over my shoulder.

"G...g...g..." the vampire stuttered, desperately tugging at the lasso. He could try all he liked; it would only loosen on my command. I had to admit the thrill of power went to my head just a little bit.

"Three more fingers to go, and then I start on another part of your anatomy." I tapped my foot. It had gone quiet outside, and I wondered what Jordan was up to but didn't take my attention away from the stubby fingers in front of me.

"Gunslinger," he finally spat out.

"Figured as much, but thanks." I snapped the

rest of his fingers off, and he looked at his stump of a hand in utter horror.

"Where can I find Gunslinger?" I flicked the lasso, and it released his hand and settled around his waist, snug as a bug in a rug. Looking around, I spotted a knife wedged into the post where Mom had been held and dragged the vampire with me. I retrieved it, then cut off the button on his jeans.

"You know where I'm going with this, right?" I arched a brow as I slid the tip of the knife into a belt loop and pushed downward. His jeans fell to his knees.

"Noooooo." He sucked in a breath and looked down. Already his waist was turning blue. It wouldn't be long before he was frozen from the waist down.

"Where is Gunslinger? Last time I'm asking." I'd left him with his underwear in place because, honestly, I didn't really want to see his junk, but I'd cut that fucker clean off if it meant getting what I wanted.

"I don't know! I've never met him. He has a circle, a select circle, and they pass on his orders."

"Who told you that he wants my dad, and where can I find him?"

"Nick. Nick told me. He's one of the inner circle.

Hangs out at Stanley's."

"Oh. Right. Well, that was remarkably easy." Retracting my lasso, I gave the vampire a shove in the chest, and he toppled over. Can't run away when half your body is frozen.

"Thanks for the info." Standing over him, I slid the blade of the knife along my palm and held it over his mouth.

As my blood dripped, he yelled, "What are you doing?" then grabbed his throat and started to choke as my blood did its thing.

Wiping the blade on my jeans, I stepped over his writhing body and headed outside to see what had happened with Jordan. Only he wasn't outside. He was standing in the doorway, holding a vampire by the hair, watching me.

"Oh. How long have you been standing there?" I asked.

"Long enough." I couldn't tell if he was impressed or pissed off that I'd killed the vampire.

"Want me to deal with him?" I nodded at the vampire, who was semi-conscious in his grip.

"Sure." He tossed him to the ground, rolled him onto his back, and held him there with a boot on his chest. I'd never seen anything so hot. Striding over, I squeezed my fist a few times. My wound had started to heal, but I managed a few drops of blood onto the man's lips. His tongue darted out, scenting my blood. Then the groaning began.

"That was..." With Jordan apparently lost for words, I filled in some of my own.

"Bad? Horrible? Insane?"

"Hot. Fucking hot. I'm so hard right now I don't think I can walk," he admitted.

"What?" I hadn't been expecting that. Glancing down, I saw the evidence for myself. He was speaking the truth.

"Violence turns you on?" That concerned me just a little bit.

"No. Never. You. You turn me on. Seeing you in total control, so powerful." He stopped talking and reached for me, tugging me to him and planting his mouth on mine. I had no arguments—I was on a high all of my own. Seemed my power was an aphrodisiac for both of us.

In an instant, he had me pinned against a wooden support post, the long fingers of one hand bracing both wrists above my head while the other slipped beneath my shirt. His hand slid around my waist and up my spine, his fingers tracing the hollow of my vertebrae. He pushed my legs apart with his hips and pushed against me, the friction of our jeans causing a nuclear heat to build in my abdomen.

I tore one wrist free of his grasp and planted my hand on a steely buttock to pull him closer. He let out a husky growl, the deep sound reverberating through my bones, intoxicating me.

"Don't send me away," he breathed as if in pain. As if. I had an itch that only he could scratch. We had a chemistry I couldn't deny—I refused to examine the fated mates bullshit—what mattered most to me here and now...was him. I'd never wanted anyone the way I wanted him; I craved him; beyond anything I'd ever craved before.

My mouth against his, I said the words. "I won't." This was as close as I'd get to commitment. He took it. Pressing against me, his hips rocking against mine, he kissed me like I'd never been kissed before. It was like every fantasy I'd ever had finally come to life. Reaching up, I tangled my fingers in his hair, pulling him closer, kissing him deeper. He returned my kiss enthusiastically. One hand sought out the weight of my breast, coaxing my nipple to attention with a thumb. His mouth, so hot against mine, left to suckle the crest, and only then did I realize he'd removed my shirt and released both breasts from their confines.

The blistering heat of his kiss engulfed me as he sucked my breast. My nipple tightened under his ministrations, hardening so fast the jolt of ecstasy was overwhelming. Each time he drew on a pink crest, I felt a cutting bite of arousal lance through me. I looked down at him as he kneaded and suckled, his exquisite mouth beautiful against my pale flesh. His hands were everywhere, as were mine. I wanted him with every spark of my being, and if that growl in my ear was anything to go by, he felt the same way.

His mouth returned to mine, and I wrapped my arms around his head as he laid me back, easing me onto the ground. I reached between us and caressed the hardness his jeans could barely contain. He sucked in a sharp breath. The air it stirred suddenly cool against my lips, causing another wave of raw desire to ripple through me. Before I knew it, he had peeled off my jeans. How he managed that stuff without me noticing amazed me, but I lay on the ground, naked, gasping when, without the slightest hesitation, he entered me in one long stroke.

I seized and clutched him to me, the sharp spike of need obliterating my self-control. He stayed there, buried deep, allowing my body to adjust to his fullness until I grabbed handfuls of hair, bit his shoulder, and shoved my hips against his, forcing him deeper.

He growled against my ear, wrapped one arm under a knee, and drove into me again and again with quick, short bursts, causing the heat in my abdomen to swell, swirl, and churn, building with each thrust. My nipples were sensitive where they rubbed against his chest with each thrust, doing their part to bring me to the edge.

I dug my nails into his flesh, urging him faster, begging him not to stop. To never stop. I buried my face in the crook of his neck as the fever inside me rose and burst like a floodtide crashing through a dam. Jordan growled again as his own climax shuddered through him. He trembled against me, his release just as powerful as mine, just as intoxicating. He held on to me so tight it was almost painful and served only to send the crest of my orgasm higher. I rode it, reveling in the exhilaration that flooded my body and soul until ever so gently it ebbed, dissipating completely over the span of several heartbeats.

As my senses slowly returned, I realized that the heat I was experiencing wasn't just the passion between Jordan and me. All around us, the barn burned. *Oops.*

FIFTEEN

"And then she just lassoed the fucker with fire!" Tyler was holding center court, filling in Cameron, Paige, and Cody on everything that had happened that afternoon.

"But how?" Paige asked. "How did you know how to do it?"

"Actually, it was really easy…" I shrugged. "I just thought about it, and it happened."

"For real?" Cory's eyes were wide with wonder. Paige had retrieved the fire slinger book and flipped to the pages where we'd seen the fire lasso and the blue fire of ice. Jordan had volunteered to operate the grill while Tyler and I brought everyone up to speed. Well, mostly Tyler. I had other things on my mind—like the hotter-than-hot sex I'd just had with Jordan.

Leaving the others to practice conjuring their newfound skills, I sauntered over to where Jordan was monitoring the steaks.

"You okay?" he asked when I stepped up next to him.

"Fine." I nodded, feeling awkward. Jordan had been right. I was a hit-it and quit-it-type girl. I wasn't used to having conversations *after* the fact. But with Jordan, I had no option. He was here, in my home, with my family. And the other little fact that was niggling away at me, and I didn't want to face, let alone admit, was that I liked it. I liked that he was here with me. The thought terrified me. Was he right about the fated mate thing? Had I sealed my own fate by sleeping with him?

"Will you stop?" he murmured, voice low so the others couldn't hear us. Not that they were interested in us at all. They were all on what was left of the back lawn, waving around fire lassoes. Bear was napping on the deck. And I'd been right— everyone could see him.

"Stop what?" Geez, now what had I done?

"Worrying. Stop worrying. I can see the cogs turning from here."

Blowing out a sigh, I raised my beer bottle to my lips and took a swig. Stop worrying. Right. Like I could turn it off so easily. If only I had a switch I could flick, that'd be awesome. I was so caught up in bitching about not worrying that I didn't see him move, so it took me by surprise when my face was cupped in his big hands, and his mouth was on mine.

It did the trick, though. I stopped worrying. Now my worry turned to red-hot lust. Curling my arms around his neck, beer bottle dangling from my fingers, I kissed him back, giving him everything. No holding back, no secrets, no games.

We finally broke apart when the others noticed us and started hollering and hooting and shouting to *get a room*. Oh, I had a room, and it was just upstairs, and I wanted desperately to drag this handsome lawman up there and strip him naked... but apparently, the steaks were burning.

"That's better." He chuckled, ending the kiss and turning his attention back to the grill. I saluted my family and took their good-natured teasing in stride, joining them and letting my heightened energy burn off with lasso practice.

"Just a warning to y'all," I called out to them, "if you decide to give the whole-body burning experience a try, it will burn your clothes off, and I, for one, do not want to see any of you naked. You've been warned."

Dinner was a loud and rambunctious affair. Cam had cleaned off the old wooden picnic table, Paige had dug out a tablecloth and placed some candles on it, and we'd sat down to eat at sunset with much laughter and frivolity. Stomach full, I sat back and watched the activity around me, a strange feeling inside. I placed a hand over my heart for a second, examining the feeling. I was...happy. My heart was full. Right now, at this moment, my heart was full. It was a feeling I'd never felt before. It was euphoric and frightening, and my eyes glassed over.

"Hey." Jordan's hand curled around mine, and I turned to look at him. He'd sat next to me. Our thighs had pressed together all evening, and I'd decided it was one of the best feelings in the world. I wanted more of this. The thought alone scared the shit out of me. What was happening to me?

"I'm okay. I think I'm happy," I whispered, resting my head briefly on his shoulder.

"You think?" He chuckled, dropping a kiss on the top of my head.

"It's a foreign thing, okay?" I protested half-heartedly. "I've had moments in Alaska where I've felt…satisfied. I've stood and watched the aurora borealis and been awed by Mother Nature herself. I've withstood twenty-four hours of daylight during an Alaskan summer and mere hours of light during winter—all of it amazing. But this?" I indicated the people sitting around the table. "I don't remember ever feeling like this. Complete."

"I'm sorry." He sounded miserable, and I frowned at him.

"You're sorry that I'm happy?"

"No." He chuckled, shaking his head. "I'm sorry that this is the first time you've felt that way, that a simple family barbeque is something so unique to you. You should have grown up with this."

"Oh, we had family get-togethers, don't get me wrong," I assured him.

"It's just that she was always in trouble for something," Cameron chimed in.

"Pretty much," I agreed. "I was usually sent to my room early or made to go and sit in the car if we were at someone else's house."

"Usually because you'd flick food at whoever was sitting opposite you," Tyler added.

"You knuckleheads would goad me into it, and I wasn't smart enough to ignore you. Pulling faces at me, flipping me the bird. You'd never get caught because it was expected of me to misbehave." I laughed, remembering many a dinnertime with my brothers goading me into throwing a pea at them or flicking a spoonful of mashed potatoes across the table.

"Dad really did keep a close eye on you," Cam said.

"Speaking of Dad...do any of you know where he is? Tyler said he wasn't home when he took Mom back." Rather than leaving her home alone, traumatized, Tyler had taken her to Uncle Glenn and Aunt Martha's house, Veronica and Travis's parents. Aunt Martha was a nurse, and we figured Mom would be in good hands. She hadn't been seriously injured in the kidnapping, aside from a laceration to her forehead when the vampires knocked her head against the car when they took her.

Cam and Tyler both shook their heads. "I've tried his cell. Nothing."

I looked at Jordan, wondering if I should tell them what the vampire had told me—that they'd taken Mom to lure Dad to them. I still hadn't told them about the file Grandpa had on him. I wasn't sure if I ever would.

"Maybe he took a job out of town?" Tyler suggested. Dad worked in construction. He'd been hands-on, starting as a laborer and working his way up the chain while he studied architecture on the side. Now he worked mainly in an office in Maxxan, specializing in renovating old buildings into something new.

"I called his office," I said. "They told me he'd taken some leave time."

"That's weird." Cam looked at Tyler, then back at me. "Why wouldn't Dad tell Mom? And if he's gone away for a few days, why not take her with him? Is everything okay with those two?"

"You think they're having marital problems?" It was Tyler who suggested it. It wouldn't surprise me if they were. Dad always overrode Mom in everything; it was his way or no way. But Mom had stayed with him, loved him despite his assholish douchery, so why break up now? And it wasn't Mom who'd left, but Dad. It didn't make sense, and I didn't buy it for a moment.

"I'll see if my mom and dad know anything," Cory offered. "Maybe Uncle Frank said something to them." It couldn't hurt, but I didn't think it would amount to anything. Dad was involved in something. I was reasonably sure of it now. Everything that had happened was too coincidental.

"Raelene."

I sat up in bed, hand to my chest. Who was here? Who had called my name?

"Grandpa?" I swore it had been his voice that I'd heard. The room was illuminated by the moonlight shining through the window, yet I couldn't see anyone.

"Rae. Sugarplum." It was definitely Grandpa—he was the only one who'd ever called me Sugarplum. Sliding out of bed, I tilted my head and listened intently.

"Where are you, Grandpa?" I wasn't afraid, but maybe I should have been. I mean—ghosts? But considering I had a hellhound as a pet, I didn't think being visited by the spirit of my grandfather was anything to be scared of.

"Rae." This time it sounded like he was on the other side of my bedroom door. Opening the door, I stepped out into the hallway. There! I caught a glimpse of a shadow, a blur out of the corner of my eye. I followed. Downstairs, he had to have gone downstairs.

"Grandpa?" I called, my bare feet making no sound as I made my way down the stairs. It was dark, the moonlight not reaching this part of the house. I flicked the light switch, and a dull yellow light illuminated the passageway running through the center of the house.

Hearing a creak coming from the den, I flicked on that light, too, stood in the doorway, and examined the room. Not much had changed. I'd packed up more books before heading to bed. I hadn't found anything of interest yet, but one bookcase was utterly empty. Then I saw him! Standing in front of that bookcase, shimmering in and out of view, was Grandpa. My heart thundered in my chest.

"You're really here." I breathed, taking a tentative step toward him. I wanted to run into his arms, wanted to breathe in his scent, but I held back. He was a ghost. The chances of being held in his arms were slim.

He beckoned me closer, and I went. The closer I got, the more corporeal he became. His smile was big and wide.

"You sure have grown, sugarplum." I stood in front of him, blinking rapidly to dispel the tears from my eyes.

"You haven't changed," I whispered. Which made sense; one part of my brain chided me. Ghosts didn't age.

"We don't have much time," he told me, brushing my hair back from my face. I closed my eyes, remembering the caress. I breathed in deep through my nose, and there it was, the scent of him, the one I remembered and missed desperately. He was tobacco and old spice, chocolate, and rum. He was my grandpa. A

tear I couldn't contain spilled down my cheek, and he wiped it away.

"Ah, Rae, it pains me to see you upset."

"I'm not upset. I'm happy," I protested, and he chuckled.

"Sure you are. We don't have much time, but I need to say this." He clutched both of my hands in his and looked intently into my eyes. "I'm proud of you, Sugarplum. Bad things happened, bad things were done to you, but look at the woman you've grown into. You are magnificent."

"How can you be proud?" I whispered. "I got you killed."

"You? What happened was not your fault, Rae. Never. But it was more than being in the wrong place at the wrong time."

"What do you mean?"

"Setup." His image shimmered like a bad signal on a television.

"You're saying the vampires were sent to kill us?"

"Me." He placed his hand on his chest. "Not you."

"Who?" He was fading fast. He turned and put his hand on the empty bookcase. "Below." It was a whisper on the wind, followed by "love you," and then he was gone.

"Grandpa!" I woke with a gasp, sitting up in bed

and looking around as if expecting to find him standing there. Bear, who'd been sleeping on the floor by the side of my bed, thumped his tail. Jumping out of bed, I flew down the stairs and into the den. Flicking on the light, I blinked until my eyes adjusted, then crossed to the empty bookcase. He'd said *below*. I was convinced Grandpa had sent me a message—why else would I have such a strange dream, a dream that had felt so real? But what did he mean, *below*? How does that relate to a bookcase?

I felt along each of the shelves, the sides, pressing, searching for hidden compartments. He'd said below. Did that mean something was underneath the bookcase? Grabbing one side of it, I began to drag it, pushing and sweating until it was standing out from the wall. There was nothing beneath it—but on the wall? Five planks of wood were nailed in a row. They didn't go all the way up, just to waist height. Reaching out, I grabbed the end plank and smiled when I saw the bottom wasn't anchored to anything. A hidden door of sorts. Pushing against the planks, I squinted, looking inside. It was dark, and I couldn't see a thing, but I could smell dirt and dust. Grandpa had a secret room!

"Well. That was unexpected," I said to Bear,

who'd followed and been sitting patiently watching me the entire time. "We need a light."

Summoning my flame, I molded it into a ball above my palm.

"There's nothing bad down there, is there?" I asked Bear, who tilted his head and looked at me with his big brown eyes. "You'd sense it, wouldn't you, boy?" I was pretty sure whatever secret Grandpa was hiding, it didn't contain anything dangerous to me; otherwise, Bear would be kicking up a fuss. Instead, he was curious but calm. It reassured me. Squatting, I pushed aside the planks and wriggled my way inside.

It was cramped, the opening about three feet high by two feet wide—it would have been a tight squeeze for a man of Grandpa's size. I swung my hand around, the fireball illuminating the space, saw a symbol carved into a wooden beam, and touched it. Nothing happened, and I chided myself for expecting it to. This was not an Indiana Jones movie; touching a symbol carved into a piece of wood would not trigger a sequence of events that resulted in a massive boulder rolling through the house.

Chuckling at my childish expectations, I continued to scan the small space, and then I spied it—the top of a ladder. Leading down. How had Grandpa managed all of this? Shuffling forward, I maneuvered myself onto the ladder and began the climb down. The wooden frame gave way to rock that looked like it had been chiseled out by hand. I counted twenty rungs on the ladder—the tunnel was deep, and then it opened out into...a cavern of sorts.

I jumped down the last couple of feet, then stood and held my hand out, increasing the fireball's size for more light. The cavern was round, the walls relatively smooth. The floor was dirt, and I noticed scorch marks—a lot of scorch marks—around the... Was this a cave? Grandpa had a fire demon cave!

Bear leaped down, landing in a puff of dust by my side, and I patted his head.

"Did you know this was here, boy?" I asked. He began sniffing around the cave, ignoring me, the lure of a new scent much worthier of his attention.

I slowly examined the cave. It had to be at least twenty feet across. Along the sides were a few wooden boxes stacked on top of each other, and pushed up against one side was a workbench and stool. Sitting on the bench-top were an oil lamp, papers, and a cup. I remembered sitting on the back porch with Grandma and Grandpa when I was little and them showing me how oil lamps worked. They'd kept one on the back porch. I ran my fingers over the one in front of me, disrupting the dust covering it.

I sent a flame to the wick with a snap of my fingers, and it flared to life. With the added light, I could now see fire torches attached to handmade sconces around the cave, and I walked to each of them and lit them. It was as bright as daylight!

"Wow. I'm guessing this was your secret place, Grandpa," I whispered, extinguishing my own flame and moving around the cave. I noticed it was softer beneath my feet in the center, and I kneeled, exploring with my fingers. Something was under here. I began brushing until I revealed what appeared to be a large piece of canvas with a prominent round symbol painted on it. Picking it up, I shook it, clearing the layer of sand and dust from it, then laid it back down.

"Ceremonial," I decided. I pinched the bridge of my nose, trying to remember if I'd read anything of a ceremonial nature in the fire slinger book, but I'd flicked through it so fast and had fixated on what we could do as fire demons I couldn't really say for sure what else was in the book. I made a vow to sit down and read it thoroughly from cover to cover.

"Did you use ceremonial items?" I glanced over to where Bear had his nose up against a wooden chest. "Something in there, boy?" He wagged his tail, so I took that as a yes.

Opening the lid, I looked inside. A bunch of candles and nothing else. Disappointed, I returned to the bench, slid onto the stool, and lifted the stack of papers. Something had to be here. Grandpa wanted me to find this place for a reason. One of the documents was a hand-drawn map with an X.

"Really, Grandpa? X marks the spot?" I studied the map, trying to figure out the landmarks. The X appeared to be on Shelton land, but I wasn't sure where, exactly. Putting the page aside, I flicked through the others, stopping when I saw a diagram that looked a little like a family tree—only on one side was the name Gunslinger and the other side? Red Witch. Beneath both were a list of names, and I guessed they were the people who worked for or with the Gunslinger and Red Witch. My eyes couldn't avoid it anymore. In the middle, circled multiple times, was the name Frank Shelton. Dad's name.

"Damn it!" I cursed. He was involved. In whatever went down in Maxxan all those years ago that resulted in Grandpa's death, Dad was involved.

And the Red Witch—she was the one who must have cast the spell over Maxxan that allowed vampires to walk in the sun. Why? What was in it for her to help the vampires? And why did the vampires want Maxxan? Snatching up the map and list of names, I headed back to the ladder. I needed Jordan to run the names through his SIA database. We needed to know who these people, sorry—vampires and witches—were. Were they still around? Jordan had the power to bring them in, question them.

SIXTEEN

"Rae! Is everything okay? What time is it?" He stood in the doorway in boxer shorts and nothing else, and I had a hard time dragging my eyes from his chest.

"Uh," was my reply. Running one hand over his face, he grabbed my wrist and pulled me inside.

"What's going on?" He turned on the lamp beside his bed, and I glanced around his hotel room. I'd expected it to be a mess because, you know, he's a guy, but I was surprised to see it was tidy—no pizza boxes to be seen, clothes put away. Who was this man?

"Rae?" He stood watching me, his face unreadable. That was something about him that intrigued me—how I could never tell what he was thinking, whereas he could read me like a book. Like now, when he muttered "focus" before pulling a T-shirt over his head, covering the flesh that had me so distracted.

"Yes. Right." I blew out a breath and hoped he couldn't see the flush on my cheeks in the dim light. "I found a secret cave under the house," I blurted.

"What?" This got his attention. His eyes zeroed in on me, and he stepped closer.

"I had a dream about Grandpa. He was trying to tell me something. He was standing by the bookcase in the den. So I went and looked, thinking maybe it had a secret hiding place but couldn't find anything —until I pulled it out from the wall. There was a tunnel and a ladder leading to...I guess it's a cave— or a cavern—I don't suppose it matters what you call it." I was speaking fast, I knew it, but he had no trouble keeping up.

"What was in the cave?"

"A floor covering with a round circle and an arrow on it. And these." I pulled the map and list out of my back pocket and handed them to him. "A map and a list. I think it's the vampires who were working with the Gunslinger and maybe the witches who were working with the Red Witch."

"And your dad. In the middle," he pointed out.

"Yes, and my dad." I nodded. "Could you run the names through your database?" I asked. It was a long shot. The list was from a long time ago, but vampires didn't age, so some of the names on that list might still be around. As for witches, I had no clue.

He was already nodding. "I'll send them through now." Grabbing his phone from the bedside table, he smoothed the list of names out on the bed and snapped a photo, then sent it off to someone who I assumed worked at SIA HQ.

"And the map?" He held it in his hand, studying it.

"It's our land—grandfather's land, only I'm not one hundred percent sure where."

"We'll head out as soon as it's light." I glanced at the digital clock on his nightstand. Shit. It was four a.m.

"Oh God, I didn't realize the time. I'm sorry."

"Don't be. You can come to me any time, day or night. I'm always here for you." His voice dropped, became deeper, more intimate, but he didn't move. I watched him from across the room. I still didn't buy this whole fated mate thing, but I couldn't deny the attraction between us. Our chemistry was off the charts.

I didn't know what to say. I wanted him, yes. Did I want forever with him? I couldn't answer that. Not yet. The whole idea was so foreign to me. It was like someone suggesting I put salt instead of sugar into my coffee. Weird. And I wasn't sure I'd like it.

He knew, of course. Knew all the thoughts spiraling through my brain, mainly the doubt, though. On silent feet, he approached, moving slowly, carefully, as if any sudden movement would make me bolt. He raised a hand to my face. The heat that emanated from him caressed me like hot silk.

He ran a hand around to the small of my back, the heat of him almost too much to bear. Or was it my own heat reflected back at me? I couldn't tell, but it caused goosebumps to break out. My tongue flicked along my lower lip, and I shivered, legs clenching, a whimper escaping.

"I love that about you," he said, picking up a lock of my hair and rubbing it between the fingers of one hand while pulling me closer with the other.

"What?" The heat of him was distracting me. I couldn't recall what we had been talking about.

"So responsive." There was approval in his voice. "I love the way you react to me." His voice was so quiet I had to strain to hear.

"I don't trust easily," I whispered. "Please don't make me regret it."

"I won't," he promised, a second before he lowered his mouth to mine, fusing us together. The heat was blistering and surreal at once, and I felt it all the way down to my toes. He broke off the kiss and nipped at my ear. "You're so fucking hot."

Arousal leaped inside me so fast, I felt the world spin. I ran my fingers over him, explored the hills and valleys of his muscles as they contracted and released under my touch. I felt the smoothness of his skin, the hardness of the muscles underneath, the tautness of his abdomen.

Lower and lower until I was rewarded with a telltale rush of blood.

He sucked in air through his teeth and, with amazing swiftness, stripped off his clothes, then mine. Sweeping me into his arms, he lowered me onto the bed, then followed me down, supporting his weight on his hands planted on either side of my head.

He offered me a soft kiss, his mouth brushing across mine before showering tiny kisses along my cheek until he came to my ear. His warm breath stirred my hair as he whispered, "You're going to love this."

Cocky bastard. I moved my hand to his sculpted jaw. Pressed into him. Closed the distance between us until my mouth hovered just under his. "I know."

I consumed his groan, drew him to me, arched into him until he dragged his mouth away, panting. I was only just getting started, but it seemed he had other ideas. Evading my seeking mouth, he nibbled my neck, his tongue feathering across my skin. I sucked air in through my teeth as he sucked a breast, then gave the same rapt attention to its twin. I squirmed under his ministrations.

He explored my entire body with his blisteringly hot mouth. My stomach. My hips. My legs. My ankles. My insteps, which caused way more pleasure than I could've imagined. When he dipped between my legs, I grabbed a handful of hair and almost bucked off the mattress.

He slowly explored me, coaxing the flames of my desire. I curled my toes in the air and my fists into the sheets as he spread my legs and entered me in one seamless thrust. Wrapping me in his arms, he pulled me up until we were both upright. I thrust my fingers into his hair and started to rock. He gripped my shoulders and pulled me harder onto his cock. I cried out, wanting more. So very much more. I rose onto my toes and began riding him. He cupped my ass and helped me, lifting me off him to the very tip and then plunging me back down.

I felt his hunger, hot and urgent, raw and powerful. The air in my lungs thickened as a series of aching spasms grew stronger with each beat of my heart, bringing me closer and closer until a white-hot orgasm burst inside me, crashing and tumbling and reeling.

I'd gotten lost in my own swelling desire, but it seemed my climax was all Jordan needed to release his own firestorm. His muscles tensed as the orgasm coursed through him, ebbing after a few agonizing moments, leaving only Jordan's labored breathing in its wake.

What this man did to me, and the way he made me feel, was like nothing I'd ever experienced before, and I didn't want it to stop; ever.

***

THE BUZZING of Jordan's phone roused me. I wasn't truly asleep, just dozing, basking in post-coital bliss.

"Buchanan." The mere sound of his low, deep voice was enough to send desire dancing over my skin. As much as I didn't want to admit it to myself, I was starting to believe his claims—that we were meant for each other. I definitely viewed him as mine and knew if another woman so much as looked at him for one second too long, she'd have trouble on her hands—in the form of me.

"Thanks." He hung up and gave my shoulder a light shove. "Come on, sleepyhead, we've got work to do."

"Oh?" Sitting up, I didn't bother holding the sheet to hide my nakedness and grinned at the way his breath sucked in, and his hand reached for me before he quickly snatched it back.

"Oh no, you don't, minx." He chuckled, climbing out of bed and heading for the bathroom. "That was the SIA. They've sent through satellite photos of your grandparent's property."

"Okay." I blinked. I didn't know he'd asked for them to do that, but whatever.

"So, we can match it up with that map?" he prompted. "And find whatever it is that your grandfather wants us to find."

"Oh. Oh!" Leaping out of bed, I beat him to the bathroom, flicking on the shower and stepping beneath the spray before the water had a chance to warm. Goosebumps pebbled on my skin.

"You are so beautiful."

"You're only saying that because I'm naked and wet," I teased.

"That too." He smiled.

"Get in here." I tugged him in beside me and kissed him.

"You've got to cut that out." He groaned.

"You want me to stop?" I was kissing his neck, working my way across his chest. "Seriously?" I asked. "You want me to stop, Buchanan?" It was a low, seductive drawl, and I was impressed by the amount of lust that laced my words.

"No." He growled in my ear as he pulled me into another blistering kiss.

Wrapped in his strong arms, the warm water caressing our bodies, I found myself experiencing a strange feeling; I felt secure for the first time in my life. Part of me rebelled against the sentiment. I wasn't sure I was ready to give that level of trust to another, but part of me enjoyed how it made me feel.

"I love you," he whispered, face buried against my neck. I hugged him tighter to me, not knowing what to say. This was the part where a girl was meant to respond in kind. And I had to admit my feelings for him were growing. He meant a lot to me...but love?

What could I say that wasn't trite? I know? He was so confident in everything, including his conviction that ours was a relationship destined in the stars.

"It's okay." Cupping my face, he dropped a soft kiss on my lips. "I know you're desperately searching for words, but you don't need to say anything. When you're ready, the words will come, and they'll be all the sweeter for waiting."

"Gah," was my response. He was so frigging perfect. What did I do to deserve him?

I stayed in the shower to wash my hair while Jordan dried himself and disappeared into the bedroom. By the time I was done, he was dressed and sitting on the bed—which was now neatly made—comparing the hand-drawn map to the image on his phone. I pulled on my clothes, unwrapped my hair from the towel, and squeezed as much moisture from the strands as I could.

"I think we've got something," he told me, not looking up.

"Oh?" Sitting next to him on the bed, I leaned over and looked at the screen.

"There's what appear to be old buildings here." He tapped the screen, and it zoomed in. The image was a little blurry and pixelated, and he seemed to have a better idea of what he was looking at than I did. "These roughly match up with the map, give or take."

"Okay," I said. I didn't know there were old buildings on Grandpa's land, but I guessed it was possible. He'd bought a lot of land when they moved to Maxxan. He farmed some of it himself and leased out fields to others who couldn't afford to buy their own land but needed some way to make a living.

"Doesn't ring any bells?"

"Nope. My parents might know more, or my aunts and uncles, but given what's going on with my dad right now, I don't really know who to trust."

"You think your uncles are involved too?"

"I don't know. Grandpa didn't mention them in his file or any of his notes that I've found, but that doesn't mean a lot. He wasn't finished with his investigation. Maybe my dad told them about whatever it is he's up to?"

"I agree. We'll keep them out of it for now, but monitor the situation."

"God, you sound sexy when you speak SIA." I winked, combing my fingers through my hair.

"Come on, we'll grab a coffee on the way."

Outside, I eyed my truck and Bear, who was sleeping in the back.

"You want to take your vehicle?" He guessed.

Bear wouldn't fit in the nark mobile. It didn't have an open tray.

"Would you mind?"

"I'm driving," was his response.

IN THE END, I was glad Jordan was driving because I was sure as hell lost. We'd been following the narrow dirt tracks for nearly two hours. I knew my grandparents owned a lot of land, but I'd had no idea how vast it was until we were out here, driving through it. Jordan kept referring to the GPS on his phone and the satellite map the SIA had sent him, and eventually, we found what we were looking for.

"Holy shit. I had no idea this was out here."

When we came to a stop, I climbed out and looked at the collapsed brick building. It appeared to be an old homestead, long since abandoned. Bear jumped out and began sniffing around, tail wagging. No doubt he'd smell lots of furry critters and other wildlife out here.

"Original settlers of the land, I'd imagine," Jordan said, surveying the ruins. Several other buildings, including what looked like it might have been a barn at one point, although all that was left was the roof's frame and part of one wall.

"I wonder what Grandpa thinks is out here?" I couldn't imagine building a home out here, so far from anywhere. It was quiet, almost deathly quiet, not even a bird chirping or a bee buzzing.

"Something isn't right," we said in unison, looking at each other, then back at the ruins.

"Bear!" I called. He'd disappeared from sight but was soon back by my side, head cocked, tail wagging. I patted his head, glad I had the beast on my side. "What's here, boy?" I didn't know if the hellhound would find anything. After all, we didn't know what we were searching for and had given him no scent to follow, but Bear had skills, and he might be able to sniff out something that didn't belong.

Bear sniffed the air, standing totally still, frozen. Then he gave a slight nod and headed towards what was left of the barn. We followed. When he sat in the middle of the rubble, I scratched my head. There was seriously nothing here.

"Where?" I asked the hound, confused. He pawed at the ground and whined. "Oh. Underground? Of course." Should have known. After all, Grandpa had a secret room underground.

Seemed if you were hiding something in Maxxan, below ground was the way to do it.

Jordan began clearing timbers and rock from the area. I was on my hands and knees, scooping away layers of sand when I felt it. Wood.

"I think there's a trapdoor," I breathed, brushing with my hands. Jordan got down on his knees next to me and joined in. Sure enough, a trapdoor revealed itself. Prying his fingers under the edge, he pulled but couldn't lift it.

"Is it locked or something?" I asked, examining the sides. Jordan shook his head. "No, just really bloody heavy. Give me a hand, will you?" Together we tugged the thick, heavy door open, letting it fall back with a crash and a cloud of dust. I coughed, covering my nose and mouth with my arm.

"Look at that!" Jordan was pointing to a symbol on the inside of the trapdoor. Similar to what I'd seen on the floor in Grandpa's cave, only a little different. This was a circle with a triangle and two arrows crossing each other. I had no idea what it meant. I snapped a photo. I'd look it up in Grandpa's book later on.

We stood above the trapdoor, peering down. It was pitch black. Bear barked, making me jump, and the earth tremble beneath my feet.

"What is it, boy? Is there something down there? Is it safe?" Bear disappeared, jumping down the hole and into what I assumed was some sort of cellar or storage room beneath the barn. Then he started barking. It was like an earthquake, and I yelled out for him to be quiet before what was left of the barn collapsed on top of us.

"There is definitely something down there, and he wants us to go see," I whispered.

"You stay here; I'll go check." Jordan had pulled out his phone and, using the flashlight app, shone a light into the hole. We both spotted the ladder at the same time.

"Are you crazy? I'm not staying up here by myself. It's as creepy as fuck."

"You don't think it's creepy down there?"

"Shit yeah, but Bear is there. I feel safer standing next to him than here by myself."

"Good point. Just stay behind me, okay?"

"Sure. Whatever's down there can eat you first. I'm cool with that." He shook his head in mock resignation and climbed down the ladder, shining a light on it so I could follow.

It was considerably cooler down here. Looking around, I could see that the previous tenants most likely used this room for food storage. They probably didn't even have electricity when this place was built, let alone a refrigerator. Sturdy shelves lined each wall of the long, narrow room. The walls were rock, and I suspected the barn had been built over a cave, much like Grandpa had built his house over a cave. Smart. It smelled old, stale, and a little moldy.

Old jars and tins were still sitting on some of the shelves, and I peered at them, wondering at the contents but not really wanting to find out what was inside. Maybe it wasn't food. Maybe some mad cult had lived here, and the jars contained body parts? My imagination was running riot, so when Jordan grabbed my hand, I screamed, then clamped my hand over my mouth. How embarrassing.

"Okay?" he asked.

"Sure," I bluffed, ignoring the thundering of my heart and prickling of my skin. There was something or someone down here with us. I could sense it. I guessed Jordan could, too, for he'd drawn his gun. Where was Bear?

"There." Jordan motioned toward one end of the room, and I could just make out the shape of Bear's tail. He was sitting. But not wagging his tail. Waiting. He was waiting. I followed Jordan on reluctant feet, not sure I wanted to go through with this after all. Maybe it was best to let sleeping dogs lie and all that.

"Jesus," Jordan whispered, and I peered over his shoulder. Bear was blocking my view.

"What is it?" I whispered, craning my neck.

"A woman. Chained to the wall."

"Fuck!" I was picturing the skeletal remains of a woman, the rags of her dress hanging off her bare bones, so when she groaned, I just about pee'd myself.

"She's still ALIVE?" I screeched. Bear turned his head to look at me, and I beckoned him back to my side. I wrapped my arms around his neck and hugged him, then looked at the woman.

Definitely alive. Although she'd been here for quite some time, judging by the look of her. Her hair was long, so long it reached the floor beneath her, and her clothes and skin were covered in dust, but she was breathing. Her eyes were closed, and I wondered if she was in some sort of meditative state. Although she'd groaned, so she must have known we were here. I crept forward to stand next to Jordan. I didn't like the way I felt. Terrified. It didn't sit well with me. There had only ever been one thing I was truly afraid of, and that was being locked up in a small room and stuck with needles. It was the stuff of my nightmares. But this was a close second.

Jordan crouched and pressed his fingers to her neck, checking for a pulse. I grabbed the back of his shirt and tried to tug him back. She was dangerous. I was sure of it. There was a reason she'd been chained up down here.

"Rae." Jordan shook me off. When the woman's eyes sprang open, I screamed again—I couldn't help myself. But on the one hand, I did take a moment to appreciate the gorgeous emerald shade of her eyes —they were stunning. And bright. The light from Jordan's phone illuminated her red hair. What a combination.

"Who are you?" she whispered through cracked lips.

"Go get the water from the truck," Jordan told me.

Before I could move, she said firmly, "No. That is not necessary. Look at me." There was something in her voice, something mesmerizing, something compelling.

Jordan turned back to her and looked her in the eye. The air moved, started to swirl, like a hurricane, whirling faster and faster, picking up dust, biting into my skin, and making me squeeze my eyes closed. Bear barked, then disappeared. I hoped he hadn't been sucked up into the whirlpool she was creating. It stopped as suddenly as it had begun, and Jordan fell to the ground with a thump.

"Oh, my God. Jordan!" Running to his side, I pressed my fingers against his throat and watched his chest. He had a pulse and was breathing. I was prepared to kill her if she'd killed him. He was mine. No one touched him but me. The fury rising within me was startling.

"Rest easy, child. I just borrowed some of his energy. He will recover soon enough."

I spun to face her, gasping, my shock fast exceeding my fury. Her hair was a dazzling shade of red, her skin pink and flushed—she was beautiful. And restored.

"I assume you're the Red Witch?" I asked, eyeballing her.

She inclined her head. "You've heard of me?"

"Just your name in a notebook of my grandfather's."

"And who is your grandfather?"

"Tom Shelton." She appeared to mull this over and then grinned. The chains fell from her wrists, and she stepped free of them.

"How did you do that?" I frowned. If she'd been

able to get out of her chains, why hadn't she done so sooner?

"The seal on the trapdoor suppressed my magic. You broke the seal. My magic has returned." With a wave, the tattered clothes hanging from her body were restored.

"The seventies called. They want their flares back," I murmured, eyeing the yellow flared pants she wore and daisy-patterned blouse. Not what I'd expect a witch to wear, but then I'd never met one before. Jordan hadn't moved, and Bear hadn't returned. I was starting to dislike this woman.

"Where's my dog?"

"The hellhound?" She laughed. "How cute that you think he's a dog."

"I know he's a hellhound." Fuck me, she was starting to get on my nerves.

"He is not harmed. He's just returned home."

My heart froze in my chest. She'd sent him back to Hell? I mean, okay, sure, he'd probably be happy to be back, but damn, I'd miss him. I swallowed past the lump in my throat, assessing the situation. Jordan was out for the count, no knowing when he'd wake up and what sort of shape he'd be in when he did. Bear was no longer in the game. I locked the feeling of loss into a little box. I'd learned to do that in the asylum. Whether physical or mental, every little hurt went into a box, and the lid nailed shut. If I opened all those little boxes, the hurt would be a tsunami that would leave devastation in its wake. It would break me. So, the boxes remained shut. Forever.

That left—me. A fire demon who was still honing her skills.

"Where is he?" The Red Witch walked around me, eyeing me up and down. I didn't like the shiver that ran the length of my spine and set the hairs on my arms standing upright.

"Who?" I watched her out of the corner of my eye.

"The Gunslinger." The way she breathed his name made my skin crawl. Kinda like she wanted to ride him every which way in a very sexual nature, but skin him at the same time and revel in his screams while she bathed in his blood.

"I don't know," I answered. She stepped in front of me and captured my chin in a tight grip, her nails biting into my skin. Seconds ticked by as she examined my face. I didn't move. I sensed the power in her and was weighing up my chances of taking her. As if she could read my mind, she shook her head, a smile curling her red lips. She tapped her finger on my chin.

"I wouldn't try it, child," she warned.

"I'm not a child." It was the best protest I could produce on short notice. I frowned at myself, disappointed I'd dredged up such a lame response... usually, I could do better.

"You're *the* child," she told me, and I frowned harder. "I feel it in you. In your blood. You're special."

"I get told that a lot."

"Come." Before I could so much as twitch, she waved a hand at me. I promptly passed out, collapsing like a sack of potatoes, not feeling anything as my body hit the ground, just an empty void of darkness.

SEVENTEEN

When I came to, I realized two things —we'd changed location, and I really needed to pee. I was lying on the ground in what appeared to be another barn. Man, these vampires really loved their barns. Did they have a manual with the go-to place for mayhem and destruction being A: find a barn?

I also had the mother of all headaches. I rubbed my temples, squeezing my eyes shut against the pain. Jesus, what did the witch do to me? Scramble my brain? The institute had done plenty of that. I didn't think I could afford anyone else to be messing with my gray matter.

Hearing voices, I pried open one eye. I spied the Red Witch. At least, I thought it was her. She'd changed. The gloriously long hair was now cut into a chic, wavy bob. Her flower power outfit was gone, replaced with a pair of what looked like black leather pants—man, she had to be hot in those— and a sequined top. She looked like she was ready to go clubbing. She also looked fantastic, and I felt a twinge of envy. Maybe it was time I mixed things up a bit, wore something outside of jeans and a T-shirt.

"You have two minutes." The Red Witch studied her nails, not bothering to look at the vampire who was pacing in front of her.

"I told you he'd be here." He tried to sound confident, but I could hear it in his voice. The fear. I assumed they were talking about the Gunslinger. I didn't know how he tied into all of this, but Grandpa had been right. They were involved.

When the door opened, we all turned to look. I was still lying on the ground with the mother of all hangovers, but I managed to push myself up into a sitting position. Bit of a mistake. The barn swam and spun around me, and I felt a wave of nausea roll in my stomach. Drawing up my legs, I wrapped my arms around them and rested my head on my knees, sucking in deep breaths. Slowly the nausea subsided, and I tilted my head just enough to watch the proceedings.

"Alice, I see you finally got out." The vampire who walked in wore a long duster coat and a cowboy hat and carried an air of male confidence and authority. The Gunslinger, I presumed.

"Henry, you bastard. That wasn't very nice of you." Her reply was sweet, but beneath her words, you could hear steel.

"Business is business, my dear. I'm sure you understand." He walked right up to her, wrapped a hand around her nape, tugged her forward, and kissed her.

My mouth dropped open. I hadn't been expecting *that*. She didn't embrace him, but she didn't pull away either, and their kiss went on for several seconds. I was about to suggest they get a room—because I didn't want to watch them getting it on, and let's be honest, that's where that little scenario was heading—when they broke apart. Her lipstick hadn't budged, and I wondered what brand she used. One of those twenty-four-hour stay-put types, I guessed. I thought about asking her, but decided against it when she slapped him across the face.

His head snapped to the side, but other than that, no reaction from him.

"We had a deal." Her voice dripped ice. Gone

was the sweet tone of earlier. "You trapped me, without my magic, for decades. That was a mistake on your part."

"Sugar, it pains me that you're angry." His Southern drawl was really quite delicious, and I could have listened to him talk all day. "But some business dealings just aren't suitable for a delicate flower such as yourself."

"You presume too much." Her ice was melting. I could feel it from here. In its place? Anger. Hot. And plenty of it.

"Oh?" The way he adjusted his hat told me that while he wanted her to think he was relaxed, he was not. He was alert. Ready for any move she might make.

"I am not delicate, nor am I weak. You assume because I'm female that I am both of those things. You forget that I have power. A power that you need."

"Needed. I needed your power. That is no longer the case."

She laughed a heartfelt belly laugh, tossing her head back and showing all her teeth. I didn't see what was so funny.

"You think I can't lift the spell?" Her laughter abated, but a smirk still curled one side of her lip.

"Do you believe you are the only witch in my employ?" he shot back.

"Employ?" she screeched, cheeks flushing. "I was never your employee! We were partners!"

"A partnership that had served its purpose." Oh man, I could see where this was going. He'd teamed up with her to spell Maxxan so vampires could walk in the sun. Once that was complete, he'd trapped her in the cellar beneath the barn. I wondered why he didn't just kill her—it would have been kinder.

I also wondered where my dad fit in with all of this. I lifted my head to ask. Big mistake. Another wave of nausea hit hard, and I couldn't contain it. Leaning over, I vomited up the contents of my stomach. Gross.

"Anyone got a mint?" I coughed, wiping my mouth on the back of my hand.

"You brought the child." The Gunslinger smiled, walking to me and holding out his hand. "Come, child, allow me to assist." I accepted his help. I doubted I'd be able to get to my feet under my own steam. Man, whatever she'd used to knock me out was a doozy. My legs were limp spaghetti, and I staggered a little, doing my best not to face plant in front of them. I suspected I would have a tough time fighting my way out of this one.

"Not a child," I gritted, releasing his hand and standing, slightly wobbly, in front of him.

"Not at all, I see that." He eyed me up and down, and the appreciative gleam in his eye told me he liked what he saw. *Oh boy.* "You have grown into a beautiful woman." He took off his hat and bowed slightly before placing the hat back on his head. He was ...charming. I was taken aback. And confused as all hell.

"Wha?" Again, eloquence was not my strong point.

"You want *her*?" The Red Witch stormed up to him and shoved him hard. His smile slipped a notch. I looked from him to her and back again. From the kiss he'd planted on her when he first arrived and her jealous outburst just now, I guessed they'd been lovers in the past. Until he'd done the dirty on her.

"I *need* her. She has something that will be very useful for me."

"Her blood." The witch tilted her head, her red curls brushing her cheek. I touched my own hair, wondering if I should get a haircut like hers. It looked good on her.

"A weapon to be used against my enemies," he agreed.

"You're going to kill me?" I asked, not particularly surprised at this piece of news.

"You would be of little use to me dead, sweetheart." He ran a finger down the length of my cheek, and I shivered. It didn't elicit the same tingle of desire as when Jordan touched me. "No, I need you alive, pumping that blood around your body, an endless supply."

"Why? How?" My brain was a fog, and I was having a hard time connecting the dots.

"I will soak weapons in your blood and use them to kill my enemies." He told me conversationally. "I'd only take a pint or so at a time. Enough to do what I need without bringing too much harm to you."

"I don't like that plan," I told him, shaking my head. It sounded like locked rooms and needles, and I couldn't go back to that. I couldn't. Panic started to kick in. My heart thundered in my chest, and sweat bathed my skin. I didn't feel so good and wondered if I was going to hurl again.

"You don't need to," he told me, turning his attention back to Alice. "As for you, I fear you may prove to be more trouble than you are worth."

"I spelled this town for you, so you could walk in sunlight once more, feel the warmth on your skin, bask in it. You told me how much you missed it, longed for it. Isn't that what you wanted?" Her voice rose, an almost hysterical note seeping in. I guess being trapped in a cellar for years would send you slightly crazy.

"And I thank you for your services. You were paid handsomely, if I recall. But I must confess, the appeal of being a daywalker quickly lost its charms. I haven't visited this backwater town in many a year. Turns out I prefer the night."

"What?" The whisper was deadly. I heard it. Felt it. Shivered in appreciation of it. Oh, she was *pissed*.

He laughed. Laughed! Walking up to her, he got in her face. "Oh darling, you believed there was something between us? Well, I admit I can see why you might have thought that. Your flesh was most luscious and your body most accommodating, but darlin', you became a liability, and I cannot afford those."

"I was a commodity to you? Something to be used and thrown away?"

"It was business, nothing more." He gestured with one hand, and I felt for her. She had, apparently, loved him. He'd just been screwing her until he got what he wanted. And then he didn't want it anymore. So, all of this, the spell on vampires, the rogue population that had been attracted to Maxxan, had all been for nothing? A whim of an old gunslinger turned vampire?

Withdrawing a dagger from her boot, she sliced it across her finger, drew some weird symbol on one of the barn's support posts, chanting under her breath as she did so. Then she looked him dead in the eye, arched a brow, and placed her palm on top of the symbol with what could only be described as a flourish. She had a flair for the dramatic.

There was a loud boom of thunder, shaking the walls. A gust of wind caught the barn door and flung it open. Outside, I could see the storm clouds gathering, rolling in fast and furious. The sun was almost set. The added storm brought nightfall that much faster. And I knew what she'd done. She'd broken the spell. Vampires could no longer walk in the daylight.

The Gunslinger clearly didn't give a damn, raising one shoulder in a *so what* gesture. I couldn't help myself. I laughed.

Turned out that wasn't the best thing to do. Alice turned on me, furious. And I knew what she was thinking. It didn't take a genius to figure it out. He didn't want her anymore, had never loved her in the first place. But he wanted me—because I had something he needed. The best way to hurt him? Get rid of me. Then he'd be pissed. Then he'd feel pain. Unfortunately, so would I. I didn't like where this was going.

I summoned a fireball, glanced at my palm, and swore a blue streak when I saw a ping-pong ball-sized fireball. Damn it. She'd zapped my power. Had probably drained me like she'd done to Jordan. I hoped he was okay. I wondered if he was awake and if he was looking for me. I could sure use a rescue party right about now. Oh, okay—I was worried sick about him.

"You think you can keep her contained?" Alice asked him, eyeballing me. "You think you can keep her under control? She's a fire demon, fool. Look how fast she's recovering."

"Everyone has a price. I just have to find hers. After all, her father had one." He was watching me with interest, but I kept my eyes on Alice. She was going to come for me. I was sure of it.

"What about my dad?" Although I knew he'd been working with the vampires, I just didn't know why, or what exactly, he'd been doing for them.

"Your father has been most accommodating." The Gunslinger smiled again. "I'm sure we can come to a similar arrangement."

"Such as?"

"Name it," he offered.

"What did my father want?" I wasn't interested in any deal the Gunslinger had to offer. I *did* want to know what my father was involved with, though.

"Money." The Gunslinger shrugged as if it was apparent.

"You were paying him? To do what?"

"There is a drug that is most appealing to vampires. Your father accommodated the production and distribution of Rampage."

"What? Vampires do drugs?" That was new. And my dad was a drug dealer. Bloody hell, of all the things, I had never expected that.

"Human drugs and alcohol have a limiting effect. We craved something more."

"And my dad designed this drug?"

"Good Lord, no. But it requires a special plant, one that will only grow in scorching temperatures. Your father sourced land for crops, arranged harvesting, had the product shipped in its raw state to our facility for production."

"This drug...Rampage...is it why vampires are going rogue? Because they're high? Out of control?"

The Gunslinger lifted one shoulder. "It is possible. If a human is unable to control his urges and is then turned, he will experience those same foibles as a vampire."

"You say you have enemies..." My mind was finally catching up. "You mean others like you who want to overthrow your drug empire?"

"They try. They fail."

And I was his next weapon in that war. He was the vampire equivalent of a drug baron in Columbia. *Mind blown.*

"Enough!" We'd been ignoring Alice for too long, it seemed, for she whirled and threw her magic at me, sending me flying through the air. I hit the back of the barn with a loud crack, the air knocked from my lungs.

"You dare touch her?" I heard the Gunslinger shout. Then it was a blur as the two of them went toe to toe. Struggling to my hands and knees, I tried to keep an eye on the fighting pair, but they were impossible to track. Both were powerful beings, and they appeared to be on equal par when it came to strength. I could hear grunts and gasps. Dust kicked up gritty in my eyes. Then I couldn't see much at all as the barn started flooding with vampires coming to watch their boss take down the witch.

This was my chance. I began crawling, hoping to find an opening beneath one of the barn slats big enough to squeeze through. I doubted I'd get this opportunity again. If the Gunslinger won this fight, he'd see to it that I'd be held captive forever, using my blood as a weapon. If the witch, Alice, won, she'd kill me just to spite him. Either way, it was a no-win for me, and I needed to get my ass out of there.

I was shit out of luck with finding an exit point. Frantically crawling around, I was almost ready to admit defeat when it happened. The roof of the barn was torn clean off. It was dark and stormy out, and I squinted into the night sky, not believing my eyes. A dragon. A motherfucking dragon had just ripped the roof off the barn!

Everyone inside froze, including me, only I was tucked away in the corner, unnoticed. The dragon appeared to be searching, flapping its massive wings and looking around the barn as it hovered overhead. Then it let out a roar, followed by a stream of fire. Okay, you need to focus, I told myself. Fire can't burn me, but dragon fire? That was untested. I needed to call forth my own flame to protect myself.

Confusion broke out, shouting, and vampires on fire running around. I stayed where I was, untouched as yet. Still, the dragon seemed intent on incinerating everyone in the barn. Eventually, its flames would reach me because I didn't have the strength to run. I hoped I had enough strength to call forth my fire demon powers, though. It would suck if I died. I managed a tiny lick of fire that shimmered over my body—not the human fireball I'd envisioned, but it did the trick.

Around me, the barn burned, timbers crashing to the ground, smoke thick in the air, along with the scent of burning flesh and the tortured screams of vampires. I'd caught a glimpse of Alice, holding Henry in a headlock while, with the other hand, she held up a magic shield, propelling the fire away from them. In the midst of the battle, she saved him. I wondered why, after all that he'd done to her, why she would save his sorry ass.

I stopped worrying about them and started worrying about myself. It was getting hard to breathe, and my eyes were streaming from the smoke and ash. The wall beside me went up in a whoosh of flame, and I crawled toward it. Reaching out, I gave it a push, enough that a couple of the planks gave way, and I crawled outside, sucking in gulps of air. My clothes were charred and smoking, and now that I was clear of the barn, I drew my flame back into myself and rolled on the ground to put out any residual fire.

The wind whipped around me; the storm was

picking up intensity, and the flapping of the dragon's wings wasn't helping any. I expected it to rain any second; you could feel it in the air. That would thwart the dragon's plan of barbecuing everyone. But then, looking at the state of the barn, I'd say he'd already achieved his objective.

Lying there, coughing, I watched as the dragon swooped down low, a stream of fire spraying the barn in flames before he soared up into the sky again and circled overhead, watching. I coughed and rolled onto my side. I felt sick again and missed when the dragon caught sight of me. I wasn't prepared when he swooped in and snatched me up. I screamed. I'd been going for long and loud but ended with short and breathless, my lungs still rebelling from the smoke and my stomach still churning from Alice draining me.

Being whipped into the air and flown away was my undoing. Everyone had a point, and I'd reached mine. With all the flair of a real damsel in distress, I fainted.

EIGHTEEN

"Rae, babe, open your eyes." I was lying on something soft, and there was something blissfully cool on my face. With a monumental effort, I dragged open my eyelids to find Jordan sitting by my side, dabbing at my face with a washcloth.

"What happened?" I groaned and then started coughing and struggling to suck in air.

"Easy, easy. Here, drink this." He helped me to sit up and pressed a glass to my lips. I gulped down the water, which soothed my parched throat. We were in his hotel room.

"How did I get here?"

"I brought you."

It dawned on me then. "You're the dragon."

"I'm the dragon," he confirmed.

I punched him. Hard. He fell off the edge of the bed, holding his nose. "What the hell was that for?" he cried.

"You let me think you were a cat!" I accused. He had the good grace to look ashamed.

"I never said I was a cat," he protested, touching his nose, checking if I'd broken it.

"You never corrected me. You let me assume. Asshole," I complained, flopping back down on my pillow.

"Sorry. I should have told you. My species is rare. Endangered. It's risky for me to reveal what I am."

"Even to me? You said we were fated mates. Doesn't that count for anything?" I couldn't quite manage to keep the hurt out of my voice. He hadn't lied. Technically. But he'd withheld the truth. And what did he think I'd do with that knowledge, run around telling everyone? He didn't know me as well as he thought he did.

"We are. You are my mate. And I was planning on telling you—after we'd dealt with the vampire problem. It's the vampires I wanted to keep this from. I know you have a...temper." He said unapologetically. "And I could just see you using my dragon status as a threat—or taunt—if you got riled up."

He was right. I would totally do that. He sat back down on the edge of the bed and held one of my hands in both of his.

"Errr, well, in case you didn't notice, you kinda outed yourself by ripping off the roof of that barn and turning them into crispy critters."

"That hadn't been my plan, but I was frantic. They'd taken you." I heard the worry in his voice. I could sympathize. I'd worried about him too. It was becoming more and more clear to me that he'd been speaking the truth about his wild claims of us being fated. I was inexplicably drawn to him; he was consuming my every thought.

A large wet nose appeared on the opposite side of the bed, and I squealed in delight. "Bear! You're here!"

"I found him racing over the fields, miles away. I think he was trying to get back to you."

"The witch said she'd sent him home. I thought she'd meant hell."

"She must have sent him back to your place. That's his home now. With you."

"Awww, Bear, I'm glad you're here." I wriggled over and wrapped my arms around his neck, laughed when he gave me a slobbery kiss, and his tail swept everything off the bedside table.

"Tell me what happened after she knocked me out." He was in SIA mode, and I couldn't blame him. Maxxan had a powerful vampire and an equally powerful witch on its doorstep—the situation had escalated dramatically. I filled him in on all that had happened, including my dad's involvement, up until when he'd turned up at the barn.

"A drug." He stood up and began pacing. I could see the cogs turning. "That makes sense. That would explain the spikes we see in the rogues."

"The Gunslinger said that if you were an addict as a human, then you'd be an addict as a vampire—you just had to find the right drug." I was paraphrasing, but it made sense to me. While your DNA may change, your personality does not.

"You said his first name is Henry?"

"That's what the witch called him. He called her Alice. She called him Henry."

"Do you think you could identify him? Work with a sketch artist? The Gunslinger has been this mysterious figure that we know very little about. He's adept at keeping a low profile."

"Sure," I said, picturing Henry the Gunslinger's face in my mind. He was a handsome man, strong jaw, clean-shaven except for the thick bushy mustache, sparkling blue eyes, which surprised me because I'd thought a vampire's eyes would be dull. And red. Dark hair brushed back from his forehead and almost reaching his collarbones. Yep, I could definitely draw a clear picture of him.

"I take it he was easy on the eyes judging by that smirk on your face," Jordan huffed, and I snapped out of my daydreaming.

"I've only got eyes for you, babe. But Henry? His Gunslinger title is apt. He looked like he just stepped off a Western movie set."

"I like that," he murmured, tracing his finger over my collarbone. Distracted by his touch, I frowned. What did he mean?

"You calling me, babe," he said as if hearing my thoughts. "Usually, it's asshole. Or douche. Babe is an improvement." He winked and quickly kissed me before standing up.

"Go take a shower. No offense, but you stink of smoke. I'll call this into HQ, see what intel we have on Rampage. Here." He set a pile of clothes on the bed. "I stopped by your place and got you something to wear."

"Why?"

"Because none of my clothes would fit you."

I chuckled. "No, I mean, why bring me here? Why not my place?"

"Because that's the first place they'd look for you."

I nodded. Right. That made sense. I slid out of bed, gathered up the clothes he'd brought for me, and carried them to the bathroom. Sitting on the edge of the bed, phone to his ear, he watched me, eyes appreciative. I closed the door with a smirk.

Yeah, he was hot—and the sex was phenomenal. I was definitely falling for my SIA Agent. I'd suspected it when the witch had drained him, and I thought he was dead. The way my heart had frozen in my chest at the thought of losing him. The overwhelming relief when I realized he wasn't dead. Pretty sure he'd wormed his way into my heart. I wasn't sure how I felt about that. Still, I was prepared to explore the possibility of *maybe* having an ever-after with Jordan Buchanan. *I'm as surprised as you are, believe me.*

Flicking on the shower, I laid my clothes on the top of the toilet when I noticed my underwear was MIA. As much as I loved to be a rebel, going commando in a pair of jeans wasn't my idea of fun.

Rough fabric, rubbing, and chaffing? No, thank you.

Poking my head around the door, I searched for my missing underwear, then froze when I heard my name. Jordan had moved from the bed and was now standing at the window, back to me.

"You want me to bring her in?" he said, running a hand around the back of his neck.

Was he talking about...me? My breath froze in my lungs as I stood and listened, unnoticed.

"Yeah, I know her blood is special...yeah...no." It was difficult only hearing one side of the conversation, but I was getting the gist of it. The SIA wanted me—for my blood. Just like the vampires did. But I was confident Jordan wouldn't throw me under the bus. He loved me, and he knew being locked away and experimented on was my worst nightmare. He wouldn't do it to me. I was sure of it.

"Okay. Yes. Fine. I'll bring her in. Yes. Today." He disconnected the call but didn't move, remaining at the window. Planning how he was going to bring me in?

That's when I knew I loved him. When my heart broke. The pain in my chest was crippling. He wasn't fighting for me. He was going to take me to the SIA and let them stick needles in me, keep me against my will—I would never voluntarily go to such a place, not after being locked away in an asylum for three years. Small spaces and locked doors were not my friends. Add medical personnel and syringes to the mix, and you had an *over my dead body* scenario.

Spotting my panties, I silently retrieved them and retreated to the bathroom. Leaving the shower running, I dressed. I wanted to confront him. I wanted to rant and rave and set his ass on fire. I wanted to scream at him for betraying my trust, for letting me fall for him, when all along his job came first, that orders from the SIA came ahead of me. That I was just a pawn in whatever the hell was going on in Maxxan.

I did none of those things. Instead, I shimmied out of the bathroom window, shoving down the pain that was bubbling inside me, pushing it into a little box, and cramming the lid closed on it—in its place, an icy calmness. I'd let him in, and the humiliation of being played burned beneath my skin...I embraced it, used it to fuel me. He'd know I was missing soon enough. I didn't have much time.

Bear appeared beside me just as I realized I had no mode of transportation. Jordan's truck was parked where we'd left it, but my truck was at the ruins—or the old barn. I was guessing the witch probably took it. I wouldn't be able to steal the nark mobile without him hearing or seeing. But I could ride Bear, like Tyler and my mom had done. First, I needed to slow Jordan down. I knew he'd follow. He wouldn't let me go this easily—he had a job to do, after all.

On a stroke of luck, another tray top was parked in the motel's lot, and I scanned the contents of the bed—bingo, a toolbox. Opening it, I helped myself to a screwdriver and made my way to the big black nark mobile. With a great sense of satisfaction, I shoved the screwdriver into one rear tire, smiling grimly at the hiss of air. Glancing at his room, I waited to see if he'd heard it, but there was no movement, no twitch of the curtain. Stealthily, I made my way to the other side and repeated my actions. Two flat tires should slow the asshole down, I figured.

Returning the screwdriver, I clicked my fingers to Bear and climbed onto his back. Bending low, I wrapped my arms around his neck and whispered in his ear, "*Home*." He took off so fast I almost got whiplash. Hellhounds were frigging fast and silent, and right now, that was precisely what I needed.

"Take that, asshole," I said under my breath, wiping away tears I didn't know I was crying. Maybe going home wasn't the most ingenious idea because that was the first place he'd look. And if the Gunslinger was after me too, he might already be waiting there; although I suspected now they realized there was a dragon in town, they might have fled.

But the truth of it was, I needed somewhere to gather my thoughts, and make a plan. I couldn't hide out in Maxxan indefinitely, which meant leaving, which meant breaking the terms of Grandma's will and letting everyone down. The thought of it magnified my pain, and I clenched my fists until my nails dug painfully into my palms. Damn him. Damn him to hell.

My tears had stopped, but they weren't real tears. They weren't the heart-wrenching sobs that waited to come out. Needed to come out. I'd shoved them into the box with the rest of the pain. Maybe one day I'd lift the lid, but not today. But despite all the suppressing of my emotions, I still couldn't focus. My mind was in a fog. I knew I needed a plan, but I was at a loss to come up with a decent one. All I had right now was the idea of stopping at the house, grabbing my meager possessions, and hitting the road out of Maxxan.

The thought of leaving my family, the new bond

I'd forged with my brothers and cousins, saddened me. I didn't want to go, I realized. Which left one option. I'd have to fight Jordan. He'd try to restrain me and take me to SIA HQ in Redmeadows—I wouldn't be going. I knew if I called my brothers and cousins, they'd help me. They wouldn't want to see me suffering. They'd know, just as I did, that my unique blood meant the SIA would be studying me, examining me, hurting me.

I had power now, control. I was better equipped to defend myself. I didn't know if I was good enough to go toe-to-toe with Jordan, but I was done running.

THERE WAS no one in sight when we arrived home. Sliding off of Bear's back, I opened the front door and stepped inside—that was when Bear growled, the long low rumble like thunder, shaking the house.

"What is it, boy?" I asked. He barked loud, and I covered my ears with my hands. Someone was here. A threat. Did he know already that Jordan was no longer a friend, but now a foe? Did he sense it? But there was no way Jordan could have gotten here ahead of us. And there were no vehicles outside. Unless, of course, he'd shifted into his dragon form. But if that were the case, he would have confronted me as soon as I'd arrived, not hidden inside.

"Where?" I whispered. I had the advantage. Only those close to me could see and hear Bear, which meant that whoever was prowling around my house may have felt the vibration of his bark but not heard the sound. Bear headed into the den, and I followed. The place had been trashed. The books that had been left on the bookshelves were now strewn across the floor, and the bookcase that hid the secret cave was pulled out from the wall.

It didn't take a genius to figure out it was my dad who'd let himself in and trashed the den, searching for... Well, I didn't know one hundred percent what he was searching for, but most likely, it was the info Grandpa had gathered that I'd already found. Crossing to the hole in the wall, I peered inside. Did I really want to confront him? Did I really want to know the truth?

Bear gave me a push with his nose, and I squared my shoulders. Yes. I deserved the truth, if nothing else. I was done with everyone keeping things from me. Climbing into the narrow passageway, I made my way to the ladder and climbed down as quietly as possible.

I wasn't prepared for the sheer disappointment when I spotted my father at the bench. I mean, I'd known it would be him, yet I'd hoped secretly that someone else was involved, that someone else was responsible for all of this. Anyone but my dad. He hadn't heard me, and I stood for a moment, watching him frantically shuffling through the papers. Bear landed beside me, his presence undetected by my father. I cocked my head, pondering how all that worked, but I knew I was delaying the inevitable. It was time to get my answers once and for all.

"Dad."

He must have jumped a foot in the air. Spinning, papers clutched to his chest, he looked at me, his face a picture of surprise.

"Rae. What are you doing here?" For once, there was no hostility in his voice, just shock.

"I could ask you the same thing." I looked at the papers and then back at him. He clutched them tighter.

"I have every right to be here," he said defensively, a flush of color creeping up his face.

"As do I. After all, this is my home now."

"Not that you deserve it." Ah, there it was. The hostility was back, and I was glad. It made it easier.

"You think you do?" I cocked my head as if considering his words. "Because I'm pretty sure both Grandpa and Grandma would roll in their graves if they knew you were a drug dealer."

"What?" I figured his surprise was due to the fact that I knew the truth about him.

"No, no, you're right. You're not the dealer, per se. What title did the Gunslinger give you? Foreman? Production Manager? Farmer?"

"I don't know what you're talking about, Rae. You're delusional." Turning his back, he placed the papers on the bench.

"That's what you'd like everyone to think, isn't it? But I heard it from the Gunslinger himself. Henry. Remember him? I heard he was looking for you." I strolled forward, watching. He was frozen, back ramrod straight, head down as he listened to what I had to say. "He tells me you've been producing the crops that are used to create Rampage. That you've been doing this for...oh...at least twenty-three years."

Slowly he turned to face me, his face hard, unreadable, set in stone.

"What do you want?"

"The truth, Dad. I want the truth." Bear came and sat by my side, leaning heavily against my leg, forcing me to brace myself or topple over. Dad didn't even flinch, oblivious to the hellhound's presence. He was mulling over what he was going to tell me. I wondered if I'd get the truth or a spin.

The silence stretched out too long, and I couldn't help myself. I had to fill it.

"Why are you hiding? Because the Gunslinger is back? Why is he after you? What did you do? Do you know they took Mom?"

"They did what?" That got his attention. His head snapped up; his eyes flashed. Relief flooded me that he at least cared about his wife, even if he didn't give a damn about his daughter.

"Two rogues took Mom to try to lure you out so they could turn you over to the Gunslinger for what I assume are great rewards."

"Is she all right?" he whispered, lips drawn, the flush of color leaving his face. He suddenly looked ten years older.

"She's fine. She's with Aunt Martha and Uncle Glenn." His anguish unsettled me. I didn't know how to handle it. "Dad, what have you gotten yourself into?"

"It started years ago." He began pacing, rubbing

the back of his neck. "We needed cash. The business wasn't going well, jobs were falling through. The economy had tanked, and we were going to go under."

"So, you took a sideline growing crops for a vampire?" It was one hell of a leap.

"I thought I'd try my hand at growing marijuana, sell it to the kids in town, just to get some cash. I'd heard whispers. There was demand. Dad had plenty of land, far enough away that no one would discover it. So, I planted a small crop, only I couldn't keep the water supply up to it. The crop failed. I was out there one night, drinking myself into a stupor, wondering what to do next, when a vampire stumbled across me." He blew out a breath, remembering. "Man, I thought he was going to kill me. But he didn't. He was interested in the setup I had and offered me a deal. Grow a crop of Deadnettle for him, and in return, he'd pay me—ten thousand—cash. That was a lot of money back then."

"It's a lot of money now." Holy shit. No wonder Dad caved. About to go bankrupt when a big juicy carrot like that is dangled in front of you.

"Deadnettle is the plant that makes Rampage?"

"It's the base. They extract a chemical called

Cyncon from the Deadnettle. That's what gives the vamps the high. Rampage is just a street name."

"Was the vampire the Gunslinger?"

Dad shook his head. "Someone who worked for him. He was scouting. They knew Deadnettle needed hot, dry land to grow. Maxxan was on their list of places with potential. They chose it just like Dad did. Hot. Remote. It was perfect—and I already had a field I'd cultivated. I just needed a crop."

"And then what happened? What led to this?"

"Things were going well, then Dad, your grandfather, started to get suspicious, started asking questions, poking around. I tried to keep him out of it, but word got out...the vampires knew he was sniffing around."

"They killed him," I said flatly. "And nearly killed me."

He nodded, not able to voice the words.

"Then what?" I wanted to ask why he'd turned against me. When did he start hating me? What had I done to deserve it? But I held off. I wanted the whole story first. Then I'd drill him.

"It was the weirdest thing." He looked at me and away again, still walking back and forth, back and forth. "The vampire bit you, and he died. Word spread—like Chinese whispers, I guess—that a child with deadly blood lived in Maxxan. It makes no logical sense, but the vampires? They fled. They didn't want to be anywhere near you. It's almost as if you were some prophecy, some big threat to them. Instead, you were a kid who was clueless about what was going on.

"I struggled to get workers for the crops. The vampires didn't want to work here. The crops got smaller and smaller. I couldn't sustain it, and the Gunslinger was becoming impatient. He threatened you. Your brothers. Your mother. All of us. He wanted you dealt with—gotten rid of. You were out of control, and when you were arrested, well, it didn't take much to bribe the judge to have you locked away."

You could have heard the proverbial pin drop in the silence that followed his admission. My dad bribed the judge to have me committed. I had never, in my wildest dreams, expected that. Memories of that day flashed before my eyes—me screaming, being dragged from the courtroom, Mom crying. And Dad? He'd turned his back and walked away. Job done.

"With you gone, the vampires returned, business returned to normal. Life was good."

"Life was good? *Life was good!*" My shout had

Bear's hackles raised. "It wasn't good for me, *Father*! I was drugged. Abused. Treated worse than you'd treat a dog—no offense, Bear—hurt, tortured. All so you could continue building your little drug empire?"

"It wasn't my empire!" he protested.

"Oh, you had your finger in a very big piece of the pie. You sacrificed me for it. For the money."

"I had to protect the family," he protested.

"I was family too, Dad. Me. Your daughter." My cheeks were wet, and I wiped my hand across my face absently. "You could have asked for help. What about Uncle Glenn and Uncle Roy? They could have helped you."

"They didn't know. The fewer people who knew, the better. I'd already risked—"

"What did you risk, Dad? Nothing you weren't prepared to lose, eh?"

"It turned out okay, didn't it?" he shouted. "You got out. Moved to Alaska. Had a life."

"Are you fucking serious?" I yelled back. "I was damaged goods. They broke me. *Broke me.* Can't you get that through your thick head? *You* did this to me. YOU!" My tears were coming so thick and fast I could barely see. Bear was growling, a long low rumble like the thunder of an incoming storm.

"I didn't! It was the Gunslinger! He forced me into it."

"Bullshit." Dragging in a gulping breath, I calmed myself. Lowered my voice. "I messed it up for you when I came home, didn't I? That's why you were so hostile. So angry. Because with me back in town, the vampires were antsy again. They didn't want to be near the girl with the poison blood."

I wasn't prepared for the lick of fire he launched at me. It caught me in the shoulder, hard, and I staggered backward, clutching my shoulder in pain.

"Touch her again, and you're a dead man." Jordan's voice behind me made me jump. I hadn't realized he was there. Stepping up beside me, his pyre gun aimed at Dad, he glanced over at me. "Are you okay?"

"Fine." I wasn't hurt, not in the physical sense. Emotionally? Emotionally I was reeling. Emotionally I had shattered into a million pieces and wasn't sure I'd ever be whole again.

"Hands behind your back, Shelton," Jordan barked, waiting until Dad obeyed before approaching with glowing handcuffs and collar. I never expected to see my father in them. It was surreal. "You're under arrest for violation of the SIA law one—endangering human life." Jordan read him his rights, such as they were.

"But…"

"Shut up." Jordan punched him in the stomach, and I gasped. "If you know what's good for you, you'll keep your mouth shut because right now? Right now, I want to rip your fucking throat out for what you've done to her. I am only just holding it together. I just need one fucking excuse, *one*, and I'll end you." I'd never heard such a menacing tone, and even I swallowed in fear. It was true. Jordan was furious; it emanated from him in waves, his movements jerky, his face tense, his jaw clenched.

I followed a safe distance behind when Jordan hauled him up the ladder none too gently and into the den. I could see the nark mobile outside, blue and red lights flashing. I wondered how he managed to get his tires changed so fast when someone climbed out of the car and headed toward the house, dressed in a black uniform with a red badge pinned to his belt. Another SIA Agent.

"I called for backup. When I knew the spell had been broken, I knew we'd have a lot of fried vampires in the morning when they stepped outside and ignited. Our number one directive is to keep the public unaware of the supernatural."

Jordan handed Dad over to the other agent, who didn't so much as glance my way, simply took Dad by the arm and led him out to the car. I figured he'd return any second and help Jordan take me in. That's what they were here for, after all.

"You ran."

I looked at him in surprise. He was angry. Furious. With me? Hang on one red-hot minute! Pure reflex had a fireball appear in my hand, and he arched a brow.

"If you make me burn down my grandparents' house…" I didn't finish the sentence. I'd what? Hate him forever? Kill him? To be honest, I didn't know what I'd do, but I knew what I needed to do, and that was to protect myself.

"Outside." He pointed to the rear of the house. I glanced out the window and saw the other SIA agent sitting behind the driver's wheel, waiting. So, Jordan thought he could bring me in on his own. *Pft*. I had news for him.

Stalking out of the room, my hands clenched into fists, but fire leaking out anyway, I stormed down the passageway and out the back door, down the steps, to the familiar patch of scorched grass. I rounded on him.

"You expected me to stick around and let you

take me into SIA?" I accused. It was his turn to look surprised. "I heard you, dick. On the phone. Saying you'd *bring me in.*"

I was not expecting him to throw back his head and laugh. Long and hard. It was disconcerting, to say the least. And a tad hurtful. I felt my eyes well up with tears and did my best to blink them away before they overflowed onto my cheeks.

"Oh, Rae." He shook his head, slowly regaining his composure. Then he caught a glimpse of my face and sobered instantly. Stepping toward me, he stopped when I raised my hands and shot a fireball at him. It bounced off his chest and to the ground, where it fizzled out.

"Just so you know, fire can't hurt me either." He continued his approach, a little more cautiously this time. "It isn't what you think, babe, I swear." I stepped back as he approached. I was tired of having the people I loved betray me. It wore a girl down after a while.

"Sure." I didn't believe him, not for one second. The nark mobile parked out front with a second SIA agent waiting in it told me differently.

"I was on the phone with the Director of the SIA, Nate Wilder. He wants you to come in—"

"So, he can run more tests on me!" I jumped in

before he could finish speaking, but he was shaking his head.

"No. No more tests. They've got your blood. It's confirmed you're paranormal."

"What then?" I eyed him suspiciously. What else was there?

"He wants you on the team permanently. He wants you to sign a contract to become a fully qualified SIA Agent, which means you have to undergo the training. He wants to meet with you to discuss all of that. I'll prove it." Whipping out his phone, he dialed, then, with his eyes boring into mine, spoke into the receiver. "Yeah, Nate? I'm with Rae. She's under the assumption that we want to bring her into the SIA to run tests. Can you repeat to her what you said to me?"

There was a pause while Nate responded, and Jordan listened. I squirmed with an ever-growing sense of embarrassment. Had I got it wrong? Then Jordan thrust the phone toward me, and I took it automatically.

Tentatively I spoke, "Hello?"

"Rae, great to put a voice to a name. I'll keep this brief, but I wanted to reiterate what Jordan has already told you. I'd like to meet with you to discuss you joining the SIA permanently. Your blood tests came back positive as fire demon, so you're good to go there. We just need to do some paperwork. I'll warn you, though, you will have to undergo a medical, that's part of our hiring process. And then you'd commence training."

"I—" I didn't know what to say.

"I have to go. Sorry, Rae. We're arranging another team to head out to Maxxan to try to contain the vampire situation. I've authorized Agent Buchanan to set up an ongoing field office in Maxxan. If it helps sweeten the deal, after your training is complete, you can work out of the Maxxan office."

"Okay," I squeaked. Nate hung up with a quick goodbye, and wordlessly, I held the phone out to Jordan.

Jordan slipped the phone into his back pocket.

"Um." I looked at my feet, unsure of what to say. I'd jumped to conclusions, misjudged him, and it didn't sit well with me. I'd had a lifetime of people doing that to me, and I knew it didn't feel good to be on the receiving end.

"I'm sorry." I apologized, feeling small. But also relieved because the man I'd fallen for hadn't betrayed me.

"You have nothing to be sorry for. I understand how it must have looked to you."

"You do?" I'm not sure I'd have been so understanding if the shoe was on the other foot. This time when he stepped closer, I didn't retreat, letting him cup my face and tilt my head up to his.

"It's going to take you some time to believe that I will never hurt you, never go behind your back, never betray you. I get it. I know it takes a lot for you to put your trust in me. Believe me when I say I will never, ever betray it. Or you. In any way." He kissed me softly. "I love you. You are my world. There is no me without you."

Our foreheads were pressed together. His hands locked onto my waist while mine coiled around his neck. I believed him. I felt it, in the beat of his heart, the flow of energy between us. As much as I fought it, as much as I ran from it, I finally had to admit it. He was mine, and I was his.

This time I cupped his face and drank him in, my heart thumping.

"I love you," I whispered. The smile that lit up his face was worth it. I'd only ever said those words to my mom. Ever. It was monumental, but the love shining out of his eyes told me it was worth it. He was worth it. The risk was worth it.

"I love you too." And I had to admit, hearing it was pretty awesome.

Our lips met, the kiss soft, a mere brush of flesh against flesh, but it was all the more poignant because of it. Our hearts were in that kiss, in that gap between heartbeats, in that one sliver of time that was inexplicably ours amongst the chaos. I was his. He was mine. Together, we were one.

"We do have a problem, though," I said, my lips a hairbreadth from his, the act of speaking sending a wave of lust through me as my mouth seductively brushed his as I spoke.

He sucked in a breath and then let it out slowly.

"Oh?" He lifted his head, giving us space. "What's that?"

"Grandma's will. If I leave Maxxan, I'll lose the house."

"I do believe she had a contingency plan." Reaching into his back pocket, he pulled out a folded envelope and handed it to me.

"What's this?" I eyed it suspiciously. Was this another letter from my grandma?

"Read it," he prompted. Still, I continued to frown, studying the envelope with my name scrawled on the front.

"What does it say?"

"I don't know. She gave it to me before she died. She said I'd know when to give it to you. I think this is the time."

With trembling hands, I opened the letter.

My darling Raelene. You'll have to forgive an old woman and her funny old ways, and by now, I hope you've forgiven me for the will. It was the only way I could think of to get you to stay in Maxxan, and if you're reading this, well, it was successful, was it not?

Let us talk about Jordan. I knew he was the man for you the moment I laid eyes on him. And I knew you'd fight him tooth and nail. I hope you'll forgive this old lady for revealing some of your secrets to help him in his quest to win your heart.

And don't go blaming him for this—he had no idea either. Call it intuition, sixth sense, psychic ability, but I had this feeling of knowing that the two of you belonged together, that he would do right by you, that he would be the calm to your storm. If you're reading this letter, then know that I am smiling because I was right!

By now, I assume you're stressing about the will and leaving Maxxan, for I'm aware of what your future holds —and it's great things. Jordan has in his possession another letter—to be given to Mr. Jacobs. It's an addendum to the will, giving you permission to leave Maxxan but retain your rights to the house. Now don't blow a fuse, my dear. Jordan didn't know about any of this, and I'm sure he's an honorable man who did not open these letters.

Maxxan needs you, and I know you're destined for great things here, Rae. Now go, join the SIA, be the strong, courageous, brilliant woman I know you to be. And tell Jordan I said hello.

All my love,

Grandma

"What does it say?" he asked after I lowered the letter, hands still trembling.

Shaking my head in wonder, I handed it to him wordlessly. He quickly scanned it before handing it back.

"She has the gift." Jordan grinned.

"The gift?"

"Of Sight. She was a seer. I never knew." Putting his arm around my shoulders, he led me inside. So much to take in. Could Grandma predict the future? But why hadn't she predicted Grandpa's death and what had happened to me? I voiced my concerns to Jordan, who shrugged. "Maybe it didn't work that way for her. Maybe she can only see fated mates? I don't know."

"You have another letter?" She'd mentioned one to give to the lawyer.

"I do." He nodded.

"For the lawyer?" He nodded again. Okay. I absorbed the weirdness of it all, filed it away, made a promise to myself that I'd dig further into Grandma's past, find out her history. If she was a seer, did that mean she wasn't one hundred percent human? It seemed that for every answer, I had a dozen more questions.

"Are you ready?"

"Ready?" I wasn't expecting to go to Redmeadows tonight. We had a horde of vampires that we were expecting to go up in a puff of smoke as soon as they unsuspectedly walked in the sunlight at dawn. Which was, I glanced at my phone, in two hours!

"To fight rogue vampires?" Jordan cocked his head toward the car waiting out front. "We've got a team coming in from Redmeadows, but a kick-ass fire demon and her hellhound would be a definite asset for this operation."

"You know I love it when you talk SIA." I grinned. Tucking Grandma's letter into my back pocket, I reached up on tiptoes and planted a kiss on him that had our toes curling. Then I pulled back, nodded, gave him a wink, and declared, "Let's do this."

It was time to claim Maxxan back from the vampires.

Next up in the Enforcer series: Join Paige & Nate in Storm the Night for another heart-pounding adventure.
www.JaneHinchey.com/Enforcers

Thank you for reading! If you enjoyed this book, I'd greatly appreciate your review.

You can find a complete list of my books, including series and reading order on my website at:

www.JaneHinchey.com

Join my newsletter here:

www.JaneHinchey.com/subscribe

And finally, join my readers group on Facebook here:

www.JaneHinchey.com/LittleDevils

Thank you so much for taking a chance and reading my book . It's readers like you who make this journey worthwhile and fuel my passion for storytelling. Your support means the world to me, and I can't wait to share more exciting stories with you in the future.

xoxo

Jane

FREE BOOK OFFER

Want to get an email alert when a new book is released?

Sign up for my newsletter today, https://janehinchey.com/subscribe

and as a bonus, receive a FREE e-book of **Cupcakes & Curses!**

READ MORE BY JANE

Find them all at www.JaneHinchey.com/books

The Ghost Detective Mysteries

#1 Ghost Mortem

#2 Give up the Ghost

#3 The Ghost is Clear

#4 A Ghost of a Chance

#5 Here Ghost Nothing

#6 Who Ghost There?

#7 Wild Ghost Chase

#8 Easy Come, Easy Ghost

#9 Life Ghost On

Witch Way Paranormal Cozy Mystery Series

#1 Witch Way to Magic & Mayhem

#2 Witch Way to Romance & Ruin

#3 Witch Way Down Under

#4 Witch Way to Beauty & the Beach

#5 Witch Way to Death & Destruction

#6 Witch Way to Secrets & Sorcery

The Gravestone Mysteries

#1 Fur the Hex of it

#2 Battle of the Hexes

#3 What the Hex

The Midnight Chronicles

#1 One Minute to Midnight

#2 Two Minutes Past Midnight

#3 Third Strike of Midnight

Clean Scene Inc.

#1 All in Vein

PARANORMAL ROMANCE/URBAN FANTASY

The Awakening Trilogy

Hell's Angel Trilogy

The Enforcer Series (4 books)

Standalones

Returned

Secret Fates

Destiny's Touch

Blood Cursed

Heart of Darkness

About Jane

Hi there! I'm Jane, crafting tales of paranormal cozy mysteries sprinkled with urban fantasy romance. Between sips of coffee and dodging my mischievous cats, I immerse myself in stories where magic meets everyday life.

Once known as Zahra Stone in the world of steamy urban fantasy, I've now merged those fiery tales under the Jane Hinchey banner. Off the page you'll find me binging on true crime documentaries or sneaking in a power nap. Dive into my stories and join me on an enchanting journey!

Find me here: www.janehinchey.com

facebook.com/janehincheyauthor

instagram.com/janehincheyauthor

amazon.com/Jane-Hinchey/e/B0193449MI

bookbub.com/authors/jane-hinchey

goodreads.com/jane_hinchey

www.ingramcontent.com/pod-product-compliance
Lightning Source LLC
Chambersburg PA
CBHW051245210726
48287CB00002B/361